Ellie

Ellie

Mary Christner Borntrager

HERALD PRESS
Scottdale, Pennsylvania
Waterloo, Ontario

Library of Congress Cataloging-in-Publication Data

Borntrager, Mary Christner, 1921-
  Ellie.

  I. Title.
PS3552.O7544E45   1988   813'.54   88-2779
  ISBN 0-8361-3468-0 (pbk.)

ELLIE
Copyright © 1988 by Herald Press, Scottdale, Pa. 15683
  Published simultaneously in Canada by Herald Press,
  Waterloo, Ont. N2L 6H7. All rights reserved.
Library of Congress Catalog Card Number: 88-2779
International Standard Book Number: 0-8361-3468-0
Printed in the United States of America
Cover art by Edwin Wallace/Book design by Paula M. Johnson

94 93 92 91 90   10 9 8
64,000 copies in print

*To my daughter Kathy, without whose encouragement
this story would never have come into being, and
to my lovely granddaughters, Melanie and Victoria,
for their hard work and help. To my husband,
John, for his patience, and to the rest of my
children, Jay, John, Jr., and Geneva, I lovingly
dedicate this book.*

Contents

1. Ellie Skips School 9
2. A New Friend 15
3. Though He Slay Me 20
4. Jacks and Half-Moon Pies 25
5. The Runaway Buggy 31
6. Haystacks and Straw Ticks 39
7. Missy's Visit 47
8. Forbidden Fruit 57
9. Face Cream, Perfume, and Body Powder 65
10. Fancy Buggies and Beaus 71
11. As the Twig Is Bent 76
12. Too Smart Yet 83
13. The Big Sale 89
14. A Hard Good-Bye 95
15. Ellie's Own Room 101
16. Susie Glick Stops In 108
17. Commotion in the Henhouse 115
18. A Broken Circle 123

19. Baptism Sunday 130
20. Ellie's Wedding Day 137
21. An Unexpected Visitor 147
22. The Dawdy Haus 158

The Author 167

1
Ellie
Skips School

She was only a little girl, but already she felt the sting of being different. You see, Ellie Maust was born into an Amish home. Her life had been very sheltered until she entered the first grade of school. Even now she would like to forget that horrible day.

"Mama," she cried, "I'm not going back." And in her German dialect, with tears streaming down her face, she began to enumerate all the sorrows of the day. "I was the only girl who wore a cap and black stockings. They called me names and made fun of me."

"Oh, Ellie," said her mother, "we are God's people, and the Bible says we must endure such things for his sake."

But Ellie didn't care. She didn't want to do what the Bible said if it made her so miserable. They had called her "bandy legs" and "dumb Dutch." And one little boy, who sat behind her in class, tried to pull the black cap off her head. If only they lived closer to the main Amish settlement, then she could go to Little Oaks School, where some of her Amish church friends were going. But her papa had made a good buy on a farm over toward Hatfield. He just couldn't pass up such an opportunity.

"Ach, Jake," her mother had said, "are you sure we are doing the right thing? It's such a long way to church."

"Then we start early," Jake answered in his deep tone of voice.

"But who will the children play with so far from our community?"

"Play!" boomed Papa. "They will have plenty to do on the big farm. No need for play." That settled that.

And now that Ellie had found other children at school, they only made fun of her and didn't seem to want to play. No, it was fixed in her mind—she would not go back. Life had never seemed so cruel.

"Ellie, the wood box is empty. Hurry now and bring in some kindling, so I can get supper started." Her mother's request broke into Ellie's thoughts, and she started for the woodpile. The oldest of five children (the youngest ones were twins), Ellie had been taught to obey without question. Her parents were good to her and provided well for their little family, but they did not tolerate dawdling.

The children soon learned, too, that you did not talk back or try to reason your way; Mama's and Papa's words were law. Ellie knew this and generally obeyed. Yet she was a strong-willed child and was sometimes taken to the woodshed, where it was made clear what was expected of her. So as she worked at filling the woodbox, setting the table, running errands to the basement and fruit cellar for her mother, and caring for her twin sisters, a plan was forming in her head.

"Tomorrow I will act sick; yes, that is what I will do. Then I won't have to go back to school." Child that she was, she didn't think beyond tomorrow.

It seemed the evening passed much more pleasantly, now that she had solved her big problem. She didn't even mind giving in to her two younger brothers so they could have the kerosine lamp in their room all night. She was old enough now to sleep in the dark, her papa said. The Amish do not have electricity or telephones or any modern conveniences in their homes. It's worldly, and Ellie's family did not practice worldly ways.

Ellie snuggled way down under the quilt. She felt cozy and good all over. How soon morning came! As usual, Ellie started to jump out of bed when Papa called. But she remembered her plan and turned over to go back to sleep. She heard her brothers run downstairs. Before long she heard the stairway door open. Papa's voice boomed, "Ellie, come now, or I will come up there."

Ellie trembled, but she stuck to her plan. Soon she heard heavy footsteps on the stairs, then in the hallway, and now in her room.

"What is the matter with you? Why don't you come when you are called?"

"Oh, Papa, I don't feel good," she replied.

"You were alright last night. I wonder when this

started. Well, I guess I'd better let Mom take a look at you. She knows better about such things than I do." And with that, he clomped downstairs again, his big work shoes making great thuds all the way.

Mama rushed upstairs. Her face was full of concern. What could be wrong? Her daughter had been fine the evening before. In fact, Mama thought, she was extra cheerful during supper and sang while helping with the dishes.

"What's wrong, Ellie. Where do you hurt?"

"My head," she said.

Mother felt her forehead. "You don't feel hot. I don't think you have a fever. Does your stomach hurt?"

"Oh, yes, my stomach and my back."

"Don't tell me you are starting with the flu," said Mama. "Ach, I shall give you a good dose of castor oil. You stay upstairs now. I don't want the other children to get sick yet, too." And Mother went to fetch the medicine.

Castor oil! Now Ellie began to wish she hadn't pretended to be sick. She hated castor oil. It tasted awful. If only she could think up some way to get out of this dilemma. But before a plan could even begin to form in her head, her mother was back with a big tablespoon and the oil.

"Open wide," she said, as she brought the brimming spoonful toward Ellie's mouth. Ellie ducked her head under the quilt and covered her mouth with her hands.

"Ellie," said her mother, "either take this or I will go get your father."

That was all that needed to be said. Ellie knew if her papa became involved, she would have to take the medicine and a punishment besides.

"There, now," Mother said as she tucked the covers around her child, "a good cleaning out never hurt anybody."

The little girl knew what Mama was referring to. Sure enough, within an hour Ellie began her numerous trips to the little house out back. Too bad indoor plumbing was worldly, too. She didn't like to spend so much time out there. Even though her mother kept it whitewashed, with a bucket of lime handy to repel the odors, big ugly spiders lived there, and sometimes wasps tried to build under the roof.

The day was growing warmer. Time seemed to stand still. Ellie was hungry, but all she was allowed that day was tea and toast. At suppertime she said she was feeling a lot better, but Mom thought it best if she still ate light. She would have welcomed a chance now to take care of the twins, but that was forbidden, too, "lest they catch whatever you have, or had," her mother said. It seemed by now Ellie's mother suspected something was amiss, yet she was going to treat her daughter as if she really were ill.

It was a long night. Sleep just didn't want to come. Generally Ellie jumped in bed, tired from the day's activities, and was soon in dreamland. But tonight was different. She had slept some during the day, and now that everything was quiet and dark, she began to feel pangs of guilt at what she had done.

Finally, she uttered the lines of her little German

prayer: *"Jesu hör dein kleines Kind, vergib mir alle meine Sünd."* ("Jesus, hear your little child, forgive all my sins.")

Then, burying her head in her pillow, she fell asleep.

2

A New Friend

Ellie first saw her standing by the bushes at the far corner of the schoolhouse. A bright flash of yellow caught her eye through the group of taunting children around her. It appeared as though a wisp of a girl had been pushed against the hedge wall and now cringed there defenselessly. "Clodhopper" and "hopalong" were some of the names being hurled at the cowering child. Just then the teacher made an unexpected appearance, and the group of naughty children scattered. Ellie remained quietly where she had been standing. The little girl in the bright yellow dress came slowly toward her.

For the first time, Ellie saw the child was crippled. Her little feet were encased in shoes which looked far too heavy for one so small. One shoe had pieces of steel fastened to each side and continuing up the leg. Leather straps held the steel pieces in place. Without meaning to, Ellie stared at this contraption. It was a leg brace, but she had never seen anything like it before. The two girls could do no more than look at each other, when the school bell rang, calling them inside.

Two things Ellie liked about school were its drinking fountains and its indoor plumbing. It seemed like some kind of magic to be able to get water by merely pushing a button. She waited at the end of the line for a drink and then took her seat.

"Everyone get out your number books," Miss Olive said. All the children had made number books from colorful construction paper which their teacher had provided.

Miss Olive was a very plain-looking person. Her hair was beginning to gray. It seemed her glasses never stayed up on her nose, and she looked out over them more than through them. But Ellie thought she was beautiful.

There was a shuffle and rustle of feet, hands, and paper as books were taken from desks and placed in front of each student.

"Today we will practice writing from ten to twenty again. Try to stay within the lines. You will be checked on neatness, as well as knowledge of your numbers." What did *knowledge* mean? Oh, if only Teacher wouldn't use such hard words. Ellie still had trouble speaking English, so she wished Miss Olive would speak just plain words.

Well, anyway, she was going to try to get every number right and do her very neatest work. She had been taught at home that work half done must be redone. As Mother always said, "Might as well do it right the first time. It wastes time to do it over again." So Ellie bent over her paper and began to work hard.

Fifteen minutes passed.

"Please pass your number books to the front of your row," said the teacher. "While I'm checking your books, you may color page twelve in your *ABC Learn and Do* folders."

The picture on page twelve was of a baby lamb in a meadow. The letter for today was "L." A little girl was feeding milk to the lamb from a bottle. A lake ran through the meadow, and pretty flowers grew all around. Right away, Ellie picked up her yellow crayon and began to color the dress on the little girl in the picture yellow. All of a sudden, she thought, *Why, this is the little crippled girl in my picture— only she is not crippled now.* She began to look at the girl in the second seat, two rows across from her, and then back to the picture of the girl in her folder. Yes, they looked very much alike. The shape of the chin, the little nose slightly uptilted, and even the hair falling down around the shoulders.

Ellie was delighted. She finished the yellow dress, then did the hair a light brown, and the eyes had to be blue—the blue of summer skies. Oh, it was the most beautiful picture, and she would keep it forever. She did not have pictures at home because her parents believed pictures were wrong. No wonder that every gaily colored object, every picture and book, fascinated Ellie. A whole new world was opening up for her.

When all the pictures were finished, they were

collected and put on display above the chalkboard. These provided many happy moments for the little Amish child as she studied each one intently. One especially caught her attention, and she kept coming back to it again and again. The girl in the picture was wearing a drab brown dress, very much like the shade of her own. Who would want to put such a plain dress on such a pretty girl? The picture is colored so neatly, too. *It looks like my old brown dress. Oh, I know, someone did it to make fun of me.* With these thoughts racing through her mind, she was hardly aware that Miss Olive was speaking until she heard her name called.

"Ellie Maust, please come to the front of the room." Trembling, she slowly got out of her seat and went shyly forward. There were a few snickers and whispers as she went, but the teacher soon quieted them. "Class," said Miss Olive, "I want you all to see the fine work Ellie has done with today's number page." She held up the book for all to see. "I'm also pleased that I could give her the first large gold star. Some of you did well and were given a blue star, some received a red star for work that was fair, but Ellie did very well, and I'm proud of her. If she can do it, some of you can, too. Let's all try just a little bit harder. You may go back to your seat now, Ellie, and keep up the good work," the teacher said, as she handed Ellie's book back to her.

The shy little girl didn't know what to make of all this. She felt embarrassed, ecstatically happy, and wicked all at the same time. She was embarrassed because she had been praised, and in front of her classmates at that. Praise was new to her, and she didn't know how to deal with it. She was happy because the teacher was pleased, and it gave her a warm feeling. Yet she felt wicked because the teacher had used the word "proud" about her, and she had been taught that the word "proud" meant "sin."

She sat in her seat with bowed head, wondering if she had done wrong. A little stir in the second row across from her caused her to look up. She found herself looking straight into the eyes of the girl in yellow. And the girl smiled.

The day passed quickly now, and soon it was time to go home. At the back of the room they met once more, the Amish girl and the crippled one.

"I'm glad you got a gold star. I liked yours best, too," said the girl in the pretty dress as she touched Ellie's hand.

Ellie just smiled. Then she said, in her limited English, "See you to morning, Missy."

Ellie had found a friend.

3
Though He Slay Me

It was raining. Lightning flashed and lit up Ellie's bedroom. Crashes of thunder sounded and ended in a deep reverberating rumble, followed by more streaks of bright light and loud cracks. Ellie pulled the quilt up over her head. She hoped it was not time to get up out of her warm bed, for then she would have to go out to the barn to help with the morning chores, even through the storm.

Why was God so angry? Had she done something bad? She didn't remember. Trembling, she lay there as quietly as she could, now covering her ears with both hands. She hated thunderstorms; next to spiders, she hated storms. *Oh, but God made them both,* she thought. Well, she still didn't like either one. Maybe he would understand how she felt and why she was afraid. Ellie truly hoped so.

"It's time to get up," she heard Papa call. Removing her hands from her ears and peeking from under the covers, she discovered that, even though lightning played around her windows, the storm had moved farther away and was much less severe. Gratefully, she jumped out of bed, pulled her brown dress over her head, and ran downstairs. It was still warm enough that the children were going about in their bare feet. Each child always had only one pair of shoes. This year, Ellie's shoes would serve as work, school, and Sunday dress shoes. Papa was a thrifty man who wasted money on nothing.

Quickly, the little Amish girl went through her morning ritual. She ran to the outhouse and gingerly looked all around for spiders. Then, as fast as she could, she completed her task there. Before running back into the house, she stopped and pumped fresh water into the washbasin, splashing her face and washing her hands. The water felt so nice and cool, it made her skin tingle. Next she filled the water pail for the kitchen.

"Hurry now, Ellie," said Mrs. Maust. "The boys are already doing the outside chores. It looks like the storm might be coming back again. It's so dark in the west." This struck terror into Ellie's heart. She knew she had to milk her two cows. How could she cover her ears and milk at the same time? Maybe, if she hurried, she could be back in the house before the worst of the storm came.

Shep, the collie dog, greeted her as she opened the barn door. He was trembling and stayed close to her.

"Shep, go away. I can't walk with you jumping around my feet."

"Who are you talking to?" asked her little brother,

Sammie. He was in the feedway giving scoops of grain to the cows.

"Oh, Shep keeps running in front of me and acting so strange. I can hardly walk because of him."

"He does that because he doesn't like thunder and lightning," Sammie explained.

I don't blame him, thought Ellie, as she grabbed her pail and began to milk old Brindle as fast as she could. Roan and Brindle were her two cows to milk. Papa said they were easy milkers, but sometimes Ellie's arms were so tired they almost felt numb. Even the cows seemed nervous today, for they stepped around and switched constantly.

Now there was a calmness in the air, and everything seemed so quiet. Maybe—just maybe—it was going to be alright after all. A few stirrings here and there, a little twitter from the barn swallows in the eaves, then suddenly a flash of light, a loud crash, and the storm broke. It lashed out in all its fury. Barn doors banged open and shut in the strong wind. Rain blew in, and Ellie felt the back of her dress getting wet. Roan jumped at the loud noise of thunder, and so did Ellie. Milk spilled from the pail. This must not happen, for Sammie and Roy were waiting for that milk to feed the baby calves. It took all the milk Roan gave to feed them.

"Papa," said Sammie, "Ellie's crying, and she spilled milk, too."

Oh, that little tattletale, thought Ellie. Her father didn't seem to mind the storm at all. He was going from door to door, trying to close and bolt them tight. Now he looked at Ellie.

"Don't be such a *doppioh*," he said. "We need all the milk we can get for those calves. Well, we will just have to add some water to it so it will reach."

Ellie wanted to explain why the milk had spilled, but she didn't. Papa would not think it a good reason. What was it that her mother had read them from the Bible story book last Sunday afternoon? Something about a man named Job. Now she remembered. Job had all those troubles—no one seemed to understand. Concerning all that the Lord allowed him to suffer, Job had said, "Though he slay me, yet will I trust in him." Then feeling anger and helplessness in her situation, Ellie resolved within herself, *I will keep on milking.* And she milked furiously.

Finally, she was finished, but the storm still raged.

"We will wait for a letup," said Papa, "then we will make a run for it." But as suddenly as the storm had come, it left. When Papa opened the barn door and pushed the milk cart outside, the whole world looked clean and new. Sammie and Roy turned the cows out to the big watering trough and then opened the gate to the pasture. Ellie and her brothers liked how the cool mud oozed between their toes. They knew they couldn't stay and enjoy this newfound luxury because breakfast would be ready, and you never kept Mama and Papa waiting. Then the woodbox would need to be filled. Sometimes their sister did this, but on school mornings, it became their task.

Mrs. Maust was an excellent cook, and her husband was a good provider. There was always plenty to eat. This morning it seemed the food was extra good. Fried potatoes, slices of juicy ham, fresh eggs, homemade bread, and rich country butter awaited them as they sat down to eat. But first they all bowed their heads in silent prayer. Ellie did not know what the others were thinking about. All she could think of was, *I'm glad you didn't slay me.*

The twins banged their spoons for food. They didn't eat what the rest of the family did, not yet. So Mother made them baby soup, and sometimes *brie.* Baby soup was made with water, crackers, and a small pat of butter. *Brie* was flour, milk, and a little brown sugar. Ellie tasted it once. She didn't like it, but the babies smacked their lips and licked the spoon, wanting more.

After breakfast, Ellie washed dishes, packed her usual lunch of bread and butter, a piece of meat, and a half-moon pie. Then she smoothed back her hair under her black cap, washed her hands, face, and feet. She put on her black stockings and shoes and a clean apron, took her lunch, and started out for school. As she opened the door, she saw the most beautiful rainbow. Oh, it had such pretty colors, but yellow was the brightest. Yellow! Oh, my, now she remembered. Her friend Missy. She would see her again today.

4
Jacks and Half-Moon Pies

Little droplets of water from the early morning rain still clung to the school's windowpanes. It seemed as if they were reluctant to let go. But the sun shone brightly, creating a crystal effect, and everything was fresh and clean. *God is not angry anymore,* thought Ellie, *and I'm glad.* She felt at peace with herself, too.

"Children, you have worked hard to learn your alphabet and numbers," said Miss Olive. "Therefore, I have brought a game for you which will help you learn them better. Here is how it works."

She set a large, decorated wastebasket on her desk so all the children could see it. The basket contained many different colored paper fish with various numbers and letters glued to their sides. Next, the teacher held up a dowel stick with a string attached and a magnet fastened at the end. It looked like a small fishing pole, and that's exactly what it was.

"Inside this basket," explained Miss Olive, "are many construction-paper fish. Each fish has a number or letter printed on its side and a paper clip fastened to its mouth. You will take this little fishing pole and catch a fish with the magnet. You will then tell the class what number or letter that fish swallowed."

The children laughed and clapped their hands in excitement.

"Me first!"

"Let me!"

"Now, now. Wait. There are some other things we need to do first," the teacher reminded them. "This is what we will do at our regular ABC and number study time."

That isn't until after first recess, reasoned Ellie. She obediently got out her practice writing pad and pencil and began to work. Carefully she formed the oval shapes and traced over other forms and objects shown. It didn't seem to make any sense to her, but the completed work looked rather attractive. Neat circles, oblongs, ovals, and triangles weren't bad at all.

Her father had grumbled a bit when Ellie had told him Teacher said she needed to bring enough money for a writing pad, but Mother had said she felt good penmanship was important. And so, reluctantly, he gave her the money. She remembered how terribly rich she felt that morning as she carried the coins tied in the corner of her clean hanky. And how happy it made her as she handed it to Teacher. Her joy was complete when Miss Olive handed her the new writing book. Her very, very own! The first one she had ever had. It was so clean and new, and it even smelled good. She would take such good care of it.

The ringing of the bell broke her train of thought. It was time for recess. Ellie was the last in line, and by the time she got outside, the little crippled girl was sitting on the school steps. Today she was wearing a blue dress with blue ribbons in her hair. The blue dress complemented the blue of her eyes. *What a beautiful sight*, Ellie thought.

"Want to play with me?"

Ellie just stood and stared.

"Come over here," said the little girl. "My name is Edith, but you can call me Missy, if you want to. I like that."

Slowly Ellie moved down the steps.

"Your name is Ellie, isn't it? Here, sit down," and she moved over a bit to make more room.

"Do you want to play jacks with me?" she asked.

"I not know," answered Ellie. The other children would always laugh at her imperfect English, but Missy didn't.

Missy opened up a little cloth bag and out tumbled funny blue, red, and green metal objects. Then she took out a little red ball.

"Did you ever play jacks?" asked her newfound friend.

Ellie just shook her head.

"Oh, it's easy. Here, I'll show you. I'll start with my one-zees first, then my two-zees." Missy's fingers moved so fast as she bounced the ball and scooped up first one metal jack, then two, and so on, until she had them all gathered up. Not once did she miss. "Now it's your turn," she said, handing the ball to Ellie.

Gingerly, Ellie took the ball. She bounced it but forgot to pick up a jack.

"Try again. You will learn. It's easy," Missy told her.

So again and again the ball bounced, and little by little the Amish girl was able to pick up more jacks without missing.

"Now your turn," said Ellie, giving the ball back to her friend.

Missy's fingers flew again, as she nimbly picked up every jack.

Recess was over.

"Will you eat lunch with me?" asked Missy. Ellie nodded her head. No one asked her to eat with them before, and she was thrilled. The other children often shared lunchtime together, but nobody ever sat in Ellie's seat to eat with her. She could hardly wait.

After recess, it was time to play the new game. The teacher set the basket at the front of the room. Then she chose someone to come and try to catch three fish, correctly give the right answers, and then choose someone else. The first child caught his quota and named each one. He then chose another boy. This boy missed one. He also chose a boy, and so it went until all the boys were picked. Now the girls began. Missy was the next-to-the-last one, and she called on Ellie, who also had not taken a turn.

Missy had named each one correctly, and now she was holding the fishing stick out for her little friend. Ellie quickly caught her three fish, which had "3, H, and X" on them in large black print. She knew them all and called out, *"Drei, Haw, Icks."* Then she hung her head, as the children in the room broke out into laughter. In her haste and excitement, she had said them in German. What humiliation! But Miss Olive, understanding lady that she was, soon had control over the situation and gave Ellie a chance to correct her mistake.

Now Missy won't eat lunch with me for sure! How could I be so *doppich?* It's like Papa says, I am *doppich.*

When lunchtime came, Missy hobbled to Ellie's desk and said, "Scoot over, and I'll eat with you."

What! She still wants to eat with me! After the mistake I made and everyone laughed? They will laugh at her, too, if she is my friend. But Ellie scooted over and made room. Soon they were sharing bits of their worlds with each other. Ellie always had her bread, butter, and meat first. She left her half-moon pie until last. Today, as she took it from her lunch pail, Missy asked, "What is that?"

"Half-moon pie," said Ellie, thinking it very strange that she asked. Surely everyone had half-moon pies! In German, they were called *snitz* pie, a dessert, which usually graced every meal in an Amish home.

"Is it good?" asked Missy.

"Yes," answered Ellie, "don't you like?"

"I don't know. I never ate any," said her friend.

This was hard to understand. Ellie thought everyone ate half-moon pies.

"Here, you take it." Ellie held it out to Missy.

"Oh, no," said Missy. "It's yours. I don't want to take it away from you."

"I'm not very hungry," said Ellie, "and you let me play with your jacks. So now I give you some pie."

Missy laughed as she took half of the pie and said, "It's funny, Ellie. You had never heard of jacks before, and I did not know about half-moon pies. We both learned something new today. Umm! This is good. I'll let you play with my jacks tomorrow."

"And I'll give you more pie tomoring—no, tomorrow." Ellie caught her mistake this time.

"I like you, Ellie, and I hope we can be friends," said Missy.

"Me, too," answered Ellie. Her heart had felt many emotions this day, but right now it was almost bursting with happiness.

5
The Runaway Buggy

Papa was a hard-working man, a man with spirit, or get-up-and-go, as it was more commonly called. He liked his horses to possess that same quality. Workhorses should be just what their name implied—able to do a good day's hard work, never lagging behind, always ready for the field, and ready to be put in harness the next day.

But Papa was still young enough to like a spirited buggy horse. And he had one. Dixie was a pretty little filly with enough speed and stamina to outrun and outlast any horse back in the Amish settlement. Quite a few men had tried to buy her, offering excellent prices. But Jake Maust knew a good horse when he saw one, and he would not sell. Sometimes Mama felt it would be safer to have an older, slower horse pulling the buggy, because of the children. Papa, however, assured her that he could handle the situation. And since they lived so far from the

Amish community, he needed fast transportation. Therefore, the matter was settled.

It was Sunday morning. Papa had brought the horse and buggy around to the front gate, ready to load up the family and start for church. Today, they had six miles to drive, and he wanted a good start. Roy and Sammie came out of the house and took their places in back of the seat. It wasn't the most comfortable place to ride, but Papa said it had to make do until he could buy a double buggy or surrey. A surrey had two seats. The boys could hardly wait for that. Then they would ride up front with Papa. Mama, Ellie, and the babies would sit in the back.

Now Ellie came down the walk, carrying one of the twins. Papa took the baby until Ellie had climbed aboard and found her place on the little stool in the front buggy box. Papa had made it for her when she was only two. She had traveled many miles sitting on that little bench. It wasn't too bad, if the baby she was holding didn't wiggle too much.

"What is keeping Mama?" Papa asked Ellie as he checked his pocket watch.

"Annie threw up, and Mama has to change her dress." Annie and Fannie were the twins, and it seemed a real chore to keep them both presentable at the same time.

"Why do these things always happen when we're in a hurry?" Papa asked. He did not realize how many times they happened without his ever knowing about it. He tied the horse to one of the boards in the picket fence, and warning the children not to touch the lines, he started for the house to see if he could hurry things along. Unknown to him, the picket he tied the strap to had been weakened by a crack in the wood. He was no more than out of sight when Ellie wondered what would happen if she touched the lines. Gingerly she reached out and took them in her hands.

"Ellie," said Roy, "Papa said not to touch those."

"I'm just holding them so Dixie will stand still," Ellie said. "And besides, if you don't tell, what does it matter?"

Just then, the baby noticed the two shining leather lines and playfully grabbed them. The sudden pull brought Dixie's head up, and another jerk, as Ellie tried to undo the reins from Fannie's hands, seemed like a direct signal for the horse to back quickly away from the fence. The board snapped, and Dixie broke loose. She turned sharply. Now she could tell that unfamiliar hands were guiding the reins. They pulled one way and then another. And all the while there was yelling and noise from the carriage behind her. She broke into a fast run down the lane and onto the road with four very frightened children in tow. The baby had fallen from Ellie's lap and lay screaming in the wagon box. Sammie and Roy were both crying.

"Stop her, Ellie! Stop!" cried Sammie. Roy covered his face with his hands, not wishing to see the outcome of this runaway ride. Ellie was holding on for dear life.

"Whoa," she cried. "Whoa, Dixie! Stop, whoa!" But Dixie ran on across the covered bridge and on toward Highway Seven.

Oh, no, thought Ellie. *Not out on the big road!* She knew that was a dangerous place. Sometimes big trucks traveled on it. But there was no stopping Dixie now. Instead of turning onto Highway Seven, they crossed right over and continued down County Road 503. Even in her terrible fright, Ellie was relieved.

But they had not gone far down this narrow road when Ellie saw a sharp curve ahead. At the speed they were going, how could they ever get around that bend?

Suddenly, a car appeared from the turn in front of them. Dixie took to the ditch and got herself tangled in the fence, spilling her precious cargo into the grass and weeds as the buggy turned on its side.

The car came to a halt, and the driver jumped out. From around the other side came a lady, and both of them asked, almost in the same breath, "Is anyone hurt?" Before the children could answer, the woman picked up the baby. She brushed the dirt and grass from her face and clothes as best she could and tried to stop the crying.

"Oh, my, Henry, would you just look at this darling little doll! I hope she is alright."

Sammie's nose was bleeding, and Roy had a bump on his forehead. But other than that, the children did not appear to be injured.

"Where are your parents?" asked the man. The children just stared and didn't answer. The man, who was trying to get Sammie's nosebleed under control, asked again, "Your Mama and Papa, where are they?"

"Home," answered Ellie, her voice sounding shaky and strange.

"Well, land to Goshen," said the lady, "where were you young'uns going?"

"Church," said the still frightened little girl.

"Martha," said the man, "something is wrong here. Nobody would send three young children and a baby out on the road alone, not with a horse as skittish as this beauty. We need to find out where they live and get them home." His wife agreed.

Sammie's nose had quit bleeding. He must have bumped it as he fell from the buggy. The baby was no longer crying. Martha, still cooing and fussing over little Fannie, put the children in the car, while her husband loosened Dixie from the fence. He tied the horse securely, talking to her and petting her. He righted the buggy, which had acquired one broken shaft, and then climbed behind the wheel of his car.

"Now," he asked, "which way to your house?" Ellie just pointed. Hoping she was right, he started toward Highway Seven.

There had been some terribly anxious moments back at the Maust home, when the discovery had been made that Dixie and the children were gone. Father took Pete, one of his lighter workhorses, hitched him to the spring wagon, and started out to look for the runaways. He followed the tracks across the covered bridge and on toward the highway. His heart sank as he saw where they were heading. But, with great relief, he noticed as he came to the stop sign that the buggy had crossed over to 503.

"There's Papa," said Ellie, as she caught sight of

the spring wagon. They were just approaching the stop sign from the opposite direction when she saw him. The driver of the car pulled to the side of the road, stopped his car, and got out. He waved to Ellie's papa to stop.

"Hello," he said. "I'm Henry Nolt, and I believe I have your children in my car here."

"Are they alright?" asked Papa.

"I believe so," answered Henry.

"And my horse, have you seen my horse?"

"Oh, yes, Mr. ---?"

"Maust," said Papa, "Jake Maust."

"Yes, Mr. Maust, your horse is tied about a mile and a half down the road from here. She was tangled up in the fence, but I took care of her. She only had a small cut on her foreleg, as far as I could tell."

Papa frowned at this bit of information. "Well, we had better get the children home. Their mother is worried about them. Put them in the wagon, and I'll take them home. Then I'll figure a way to get my horse and buggy."

"No need for that," said Henry. "The missus and I will take them home if you'll give us directions. Then I'll take you to get your rig."

So the children rode home in the car. What a grand ride. Everyone had enough room to sit, and music came from a place in the front. The children were awestruck. Pa followed with his wagon.

Mama was on the porch as they drove in. Her eyes were red from crying. She came quickly when she realized her children were home.

"Are you alright?" she asked, reaching for her

baby, who had fallen asleep in Mrs. Nolt's lap.

"Oh, yes, they are fine," said Mrs. Nolt, handing her the sleeping child. "I'm Martha Nolt, and this is my husband, Henry. We met your husband on the way. He will be home soon, and then Henry will take him to fetch your horse and carriage. Oh, you do have the sweetest children, and the baby looks so cute in its little bonnet and white cap. Oh, look, Henry," she exclaimed, as she saw the other baby by the screen door, "Another one! Twins! Oh, dear, aren't they darling?"

Mrs. Maust had never heard such a fuss about children before. This woman never seemed to stop talking.

"Come in," said Mama.

It wasn't long until Papa came. He checked again to make sure his children were not hurt. Mama had put butter on Roy's forehead, and the bump was much less noticeable already.

Mama thanked the Nolts for taking care of her children and bringing them home. Then they left with Papa to get his rig, as the Englisher called it. They were able to mend the broken shaft with some old wire, and after a long time Papa came home. Dixie was lame in her right front leg. Papa didn't like it.

"Now," he said, "Ellie, I want to know what happened."

"The fence broke," said Ellie.

"Yes," said Sammie, "but you picked up the lines first, Ellie."

Oh, that Sammie. He always tattled!

"Is that true?" asked Papa.

"Well, Fannie grabbed the lines," remarked Ellie.

"But you did pick them up first," said Roy. "Didn't she, Sammie?"

"Yes, she did."

"Didn't I tell you not to touch them?" asked Papa.

Ellie didn't answer.

"Didn't I?"

"Yes, but. . . . " She did not finish her sentence.

Papa opened the door and led her to the woodshed. He talked to her about how they could all have been killed and what anxiety she had put her parents through. Then he paddled her. Afterward, her father spoke to her again and told her why he had to punish her so severely, lest she forget and disobey again.

Well, they need not worry. She was going to die. Then they would be sorry. Ellie was strong-willed, and now she would seek revenge for the whipping she had received in the woodshed.

Mother sent her out to the corncrib to get corncobs to start the fire in the kitchen stove to cook the noon meal. They were unable to attend church because of the events of the morning. As Ellie opened the door to the crib and stepped inside, she determined she would hold her nose shut until she was dead. Then her father would wish he had never whipped her. Again and again she tried this. Finally, in utter exasperation, she said aloud, "Oh, well. I can't even breathe like that."

Her revenge was short-lived. Deep down she knew she deserved the punishment.

6
Haystacks and Straw Ticks

Every day was a busy day in the Maust household, but it seemed Saturdays outdid them all. The house-cleaning had to be done. Lamp chimneys needed to be washed and the lamps filled with kerosine. Both stoves were polished on that day and the pots and pans were scrubbed until they shone. Pie and cake baking were other tasks to be performed on Satur-day ... not to mention washing hair and bathing, polishing shoes for Sunday wear, and any other un-foreseen job which might crop up and need im-mediate attention. If some garden vegetable had to be picked and put up without delay, it was done, no matter how many other chores needed to be done.

Ellie wondered if her mother ever slept. She was still working when her daughter went to bed in the evening, and in the morning was already at some task when Ellie awoke. Papa had said that when spring came and the outside work started again, he would try to get a *Maut* (hired girl) to help his wife. But for the rest of the fall and winter, they would make-do. He said Ellie was old enough now to help more, too. At seven and a half, she could bake pies and cakes already and was learning to bake bread. "It is better she learned young," Papa had told his wife. And Lizzie Maust was a good, patient teacher.

This Saturday was no different from all the other Saturdays, except that Mama discovered the two straw ticks from the upstairs beds needed filling. Instead of a mattress, each bed had a large sacklike bag which was filled with straw. The ends were sewn shut to keep the straw inside, and the ticks were placed on rope springs, or sometimes real bedsprings.

What fun the children had climbing up on their freshly filled ticks and jumping on the big heap to distribute somewhat more evenly its contents. Then at night they would settle down and squirm and wiggle until they had feathered a little spot just right for their bodies. The straw smelled so fresh, and its rustling made them remember the waving grain as it stood in the field with the wind rippling through it. Ellie thought that it looked like the waves on a big sea.

"Ellie, come help me bring the straw ticks down from upstairs," Mama said. "We will have to empty the old straw, and I'll wash the empty ticks this morning. They can hang out to dry until toward evening, then we will fill them. I must get this job done before cold weather sets in. It's been cooler in the mornings and evenings, and I don't want to wait."

Mother started upstairs, with Ellie following at her heels.

Mother decided she might as well wash all the bedding, too, so she began to throw armfuls of blankets and covers down the stairs. She called to Roy, who was in the kitchen watching the twins, to come take the covers from the stairs so she and Ellie could walk down with the straw ticks. Roy took an armful, obediently placing it on the kitchen floor. But one of the twins was curiously investigating the stove. Knowing the danger she was in, Roy picked her up and placed her in another part of the room. By this time, the other baby was in trouble. Reaching up, she had pulled a small plant from the windowsill. Roy picked it up and began to scoop up the dirt when he heard a thump, thump, thump all the way down the stairs. There was a shrill screech, and he looked around to see his mother lying there with the straw tick on top of her.

"Roy Maust," she said, "didn't I tell you to take those covers off the stairs? Now see once what happened. I stepped on them and they bumped me all the way down." She got up and smoothed her hair, straightening her covering and dress. "Why didn't you do as I told you?"

Roy explained about the babies.

"Ach, well," said Lizzie, "those two sure can upset things." Then she laughed. "They really can," she said. "They upset me." Realizing now that their mother was not hurt, Ellie and Roy laughed, too.

"Oh, Mama," Ellie said. "You looked so funny bumping down the steps."

"Yes, well," said her mother, "we won't talk about it anymore. It doesn't pay to *schussel* (hurry)."

They carefully brought the other tick downstairs, opened the seam, emptied the contents, and began the washing. Ellie carried water to heat in the big copper boiler. Mother also had stacks of diapers to wash. Ellie cut up homemade lye soap and put it in the hot water to dissolve. Lye soap kept the Maust laundry snowy white and clean. Their wash looked so nice drying on the line against the blue of the sky. If Ellie's mother had dared to be proud, she would have been proud of her white wash. But, of course, she must not even let such an idea enter her mind.

The twins were put to bed with their bottles. This was a good time, Mama said, for Ellie to sweep and scrub the living-room and kitchen floors. The floors were also washed with lye soap. Mother said it kept them from turning dirty gray. Papa sometimes treated them with linseed oil to help preserve the wood.

The house was quiet now. Roy had been sent out to the barn to help Sammie. They were cleaning down cobwebs in the cow barn. Ellie was glad she did not have that task. All she could think of was the big fat spiders they might stir up. She liked the outdoors, but this time she was glad she was a girl with indoor work to do.

The day wore on with its many duties, and Ellie was getting tired. Yet she looked forward to filling the straw ticks. Just before chore time, her mother took the two blue-and-white-striped ticks from the line and told Ellie to bring the twins and follow her

out to the straw shed. The babies were just beginning to walk, so Ellie could easily lead them along by
their little hands.

"Now, set the babies over by the haystack and
hold this tick open for me, so I can put the straw in,"
Mama said. "We can keep an eye on the little ones,
and they won't be in our way if we leave them by the
haystack." When Papa's hayloft was filled and he
needed more room for his hay crop, he often made it
into stacks out by the straw shed. This year there
had been a bumper crop.

Mrs. Maust did not know that some of her hens
had been laying eggs out here. The nest was well hidden, but not so well that two exploring babies
couldn't find it. And find it they did. Mama and Ellie
kept glancing at the two little girls playing busily.
Mother and daughter worked as swiftly as they
could to finish their job. They had one tick done and
started the other one. The finished one lay on its side
with the top open. It looked fat and inviting to Ellie.

"Come on," said her mother, "we must get the
second one filled while the babies are behaving so
well."

Soon both straw ticks were completed. Mother
thought it would work best if they took the twins to
the house and put them in their cribs before she and
Ellie brought the straw ticks inside.

"What is that smell?" asked Ellie as they drew
near the haystack.

"Ach, my, I don't know," said Mother. She could
see Fannie's back as she sat there, but when she saw
Fannie's face and hair, she knew where the smell

came from. "Eggs, rotten eggs!" she exclaimed. "There must have been a nest of eggs out here for a long time." Egg yolk and pieces of hay were all over her child.

"Get Annie," she told Ellie, "and come quick to the house." But Ellie couldn't find Annie.

"Mama," she said, "I don't know where Annie is. She isn't anywhere."

"Ach," said Mama, "she has to be somewhere. Look again and bring her quick." But no matter how hard Ellie tried, she could not find her baby sister. Finally she ran to the house, where Mother had taken Fannie and was now removing the foul-smelling clothes from the child.

"Mama, I've looked everywhere and I can't find her."

"Get Papa, and the boys, too. They must help you. I cannot leave little Fannie now. Go, once," said Lizzie anxiously.

Ellie sped to the barn and told Papa and the boys of their predicament.

"Are you sure you looked good?" asked Jake.

"Yes, Papa."

"Well, then, come, boys. We have to hurry and find her so we can get the milking started. Soon it's time."

Back to the haystack they went. The smell of rotten eggs still hung in the air.

"Phew!" exclaimed Sammie. "What smells so bad?"

"Rotten eggs," answered his sister. "The babies found a nest and broke some eggs."

"I think maybe Annie is somewhere here in this hay," said Papa. "Start digging with your hands and keep calling her name."

Each one began to work in earnest. Handful after handful was removed, but still no baby was found. Papa began to fear she might have crawled part way in before the hay came down and smothered her. On and on they worked, and finally the stack was completely flattened. Well, she sure wasn't in there.

"Let's take this straw tick to the house and see if Mama has thought of where she may have gone," Papa said. "Sammie, take the other end, and Roy, open the gate for us. Ellie, you wait here in case Annie is around the barn somewhere."

As they picked up their cargo, Roy said, "Papa, I saw something move in the straw tick. I think maybe it's the cat."

Papa and Sammie laid the load they were carrying on the ground, and Papa looked into the open end of the tick. What a sight he saw. There was the smelly little girl covered with egg yolk, wisps of hay and straw clinging to her.

"If you were a little older, I'd paddle you good," said Mr. Maust as he pulled his daughter from the straw pile.

"Here, Ellie, take her to your mother." He and Sammie took the straw tick to the house and went out to get ready for the evening chores. Papa wanted to brush and curry Dixie so she would look her best for tomorrow's trip to church. Her leg had healed well with his expert care and his standby remedy of Black Diamond Liniment.

Ellie helped clean up the messy twins, then made her way to the barn to milk her two cows. A yellow butterfly fluttered around a little mud puddle by the barn door. She thought of Missy. Oh, she would have so much to tell her next school day ... all about the haystack and straw tick and the twins.

After the chores were finished and the supper dishes done, the children took turns taking their Saturday evening baths in the big tin tub which was brought into the kitchen. Ellie was tired and anxious to get to bed. After Mother had tightly braided her freshly washed hair, Ellie headed upstairs and made her little spot in the newly filled tick.

"I almost spanked that Annie today," Jake said to his wife. "I needed to hold back with all my might to keep from it. Now I have to restack the hay."

"I need a *Maut*," is all Lizzie said.

7
Missy's Visit

"Ellie," said Missy one day, "my mother said if it's alright with your mother, I can go home with you from school and spend the night."

"You mean sleep at our house?" asked Ellie, very much surprised.

"Yes," answered her friend. "Do you want me to?"

"Oh, yeah," said Ellie, forgetting her grammar. "That will be fun. I will ask Mama tonight." She could hardly wait until time to go home.

"Mama," Ellie called out as soon as she entered the kitchen that evening. "Mama, can Missy come home with me and sleep here all night? Her mama said if it's alright with you, she can. Can she?"

"Ellie, slow down once," said her mother. "You rattle on so I can hardly make out what you are saying."

So Ellie told her mother again what Missy had said.

"Ach, my, I don't know," exclaimed Mrs. Maust. "We better ask your papa."

Ellie was disappointed. Now she had to wait until the chores were done and supper was over with, and everything cleared away. That seemed like forever to Ellie, but wait she must. Had she not been so busy with all her various evening tasks, she might not have stood the suspense.

Finally the time came when Papa was relaxing in his favorite rocker reading the *Farm Journal.* Mother was busily mending stockings, and Ellie was minding the twins. She looked up at Mama and said, "Did you ask him yet?"

Mother smiled slightly at her daughter's anxious look and shook her head. "Wait until we have put the twins to bed."

What! She had to wait longer yet. And, oh, sometimes it took so long before those babies would cooperate. Well, there was nothing she could do except hope her little sisters would go to bed without fussing tonight.

At last, the house was quiet. The boys had gone upstairs and were already asleep. Ellie could hear the ticking of the old shelf clock. It seemed to keep time with the beating of her heart as she looked at her mother again. When, oh when, would she ask?

"Jake," said Lizzie at long last, "Ellie wants to know if it's alright if her little crippled friend from school comes home with her and stays all night. She said the girl's mother said she can, if it's alright with us."

"Well," Jake said soberly, "I don't know if it is

such a good idea to bring an Englisher into our home. Ellie might not do her work and just want to play. You know you need her to help you, Lizzie."

"I'll make-do," answered his wife. "How can we say no, Jake? Ellie tells me the other schoolchildren are sometimes mean to this girl. If it were not for the schoolmarm, she would really have it hard. We always teach our children to be kind, especially to those less fortunate and to the handicapped."

"Well, then," answered Ellie's papa, "this once. We will try it this one time. But mind, Ellie, you do your work and help your mother like always."

"Yeah, Papa, I will," she promised. Ellie was so happy she could have kissed them both, only she never did, because in an Amish home one does not show open affection. Well, babies are okay to kiss, but not after they become a little older and are not babies anymore.

Ellie could hardly wait to tell Missy the good news. She went to bed, but sleep wouldn't come.

Next day at school, the two girls were especially happy. Missy was going to ask her mother that very night how soon she could visit Ellie at her house.

At last the big day came when Missy arrived at school with a small overnight bag. It was hard all day for the two girls to keep their minds on their schoolwork. Missy was wearing her yellow dress again. It was Ellie's favorite, and she was sure her parents would like it, too. How little she understood the ways of her people.

Mrs. Maust had been baking bread and was just taking the last loaves out of the oven as the two girls entered. How good it smelled! Mother looked up from her work and said, "Ellie, hurry and change your dress. The babies have been extra cranky today. Bring a pail of water from the pumphouse, then fix some bread and apple butter for the twins. I believe they are hungry."

"So am I," replied Ellie. "Can Missy and I have some, too?"

"Yes, if you do what I told you."

Missy just stood there holding onto her overnight case. No one told her where she might put it. The babies were sitting in the middle of the floor, surrounded by pots and pans and a few wooden spoons. These were their toys. They stared at Missy.

"How cute they are," Missy said under her breath.

"Come," said Ellie, "you can put your stuff upstairs in my room. Didn't your mother send your chore dress along?" asked Ellie.

"I don't have any," said Missy. "I just wear the dress I wore to school all evening. Then in the morning, I wear a clean one again."

"You must have lots of dresses then," remarked Ellie. She had never heard of wearing a different dress each day. Missy's parents must have lots and lots of money.

Missy smiled. "I think I have seven or eight good dresses for fancy, and I guess ten for school. I forget how many are just to wear around home."

Ellie was trying to imagine such a store of dresses when she heard her mother call. Quickly she slipped into her patched and faded everyday dress and told her playmate they must hurry downstairs. But

Missy couldn't hurry, or she would fall. So Ellie helped her down each step.

"Why must you always hurry?" asked Missy.

"Because I have to help Mama with the work and the babies," she answered.

"You are so lucky to have such cute babies, I wish I'd have even one baby sister. And you have two. You are lucky."

Ellie didn't really know what she meant, but if Missy said it, she accepted it as something good.

"Don't you want to wear an apron over your dress so you won't get it dirty?" Mrs. Maust asked Missy.

"I don't have any," answered Missy.

"Well then, Ellie, go get your blue apron for Missy. She can wear that, or her dress won't be fit for school tomorrow." Lizzie Maust did not realize that the little English girl had a clean dress for tomorrow, folded away in her suitcase. Missy loved the quaint blue apron, even if it was much longer than the dress she was wearing. It had a roomy pocket, and she dug her hand down deep inside.

Ellie fixed some freshly baked warm bread with homemade butter and apple butter for each of the babies, and some for Missy and herself.

"Come," she said, "we will sit on the floor and feed the babies their bread and eat ours at the same time."

She forgot that her friend couldn't sit on the floor because of her leg brace. So they arranged a chair in front of the two little ones and began to enjoy their snack. At first the twins shied away from the new girl, but gradually their curiosity was aroused, and they began to play with the shiny chrome on her brace.

Missy could not follow Ellie when she gathered the eggs, or carried water and kindling wood, or when she filled the tank at the end of the cookstove with water, but she did hobble along out to watch her milk her two cows. Mr. Maust and his two boys were out in the barn when the girls came home from school, so they had not seen Missy before. The boys both stood and stared at her. Then they went on with the feeding, but every once in a while they would peek around the corners and whisper to each other.

Ellie took her little milking stool and sat down to milk Brindle.

"Aren't you afraid?" asked Missy. The cows looked huge to the city girl.

"Of what?" asked Ellie.

"Why, this big cow. He is much bigger than you are. He could step on you with his big legs and hurt you."

"Oh, no," answered Ellie, "and 'he' is a 'she.' "

When Jake Maust first saw Missy, he mumbled something under his breath and gave her a reproachful look. He did not approve of her cut hair and her bright yellow dress. But when he saw her limp after Ellie as she changed from milking Brindle to Roan, his heart mellowed somewhat. And when he heard the little Englisher ask Ellie how she knew when to turn the cow's faucets off, he chuckled aloud.

Things were so different here in the Maust home.

There was no indoor plumbing and there were no pictures on the walls ... no radio or piano, no electricity or telephone, no draperies at the windows. But everything was neat and clean.

Suppertime was different, too. A big kettle of hot soup was set in the center of the table. A dipper was placed in the kettle. Then after a silent prayer, all of them took turns holding their soup plates up to the kettle while Mother ladled out a portion for each one. Missy had never eaten any soup like this. When she asked what it was, Ellie's mother said, "Rivvel soup." It was made from milk, flour, eggs, a pat of butter, salted and peppered to taste. She liked it and took a second helping. Then, of course, there were half-moon pies. Everything tasted so good. There was more homemade bread and apple butter, too.

After everyone finished eating, they bowed their heads again in silent thanks. Then the two girls began to clear the table and wash the dishes.

"Do you want to wash or dry?" asked Ellie.

"I don't care," replied Missy.

"Well, why don't you wash and I'll dry, because I know where the dishes belong. I'll put them away. Then if we can get the babies to go to bed, we can play."

"Where are your toys?" asked Missy.

"I don't have toys, but we can play 'Pick-Out-of-the-Catalog,' or sometimes we play 'Hide the Thimble.' "

So the girls worked as fast as they could. Mrs. Maust made all of the family's clothes (except the stockings and men's underwear), so she was busy at the sewing machine making a chore coat for Sammie. She was glad when the girls finished the dishes and came to relieve Roy and Sammie of the care of Annie and Fannie. The boys just were not as good with them as their sister was.

"Why do the babies wear little caps on their heads?" asked Missy.

"Because they are Amish like we are, and we are supposed to," replied Ellie.

"Oh," was all Missy said.

Mother put her sewing aside at eight o'clock and helped her daughter get the little ones ready for bed. Now Ellie and Missy were free to play. Ellie brought out the big Sears Roebuck catalog, and her brothers came shyly to ask if they could play, too. They always wanted to pick from pages with boys' toys, and Ellie liked the girls' things, so Mother said to take turns.

All but one—the one who was "it"—would close their eyes. Then the "it" person would choose an item she would like to have if she could pick it right out of the book. Then she would call out "ready." Each of the players would point to items they believed were what the picker had chosen, and would ask, "This? This? This?" until someone found the right one. Then the person who found the right object was "it," and so on.

Ellie loved the pages with dolls. When Missy pointed to a beautiful one with yellow curls and a pink dress and told Ellie, "I have one just like that," Ellie thought Missy must be the happiest girl in the whole world. And when Missy told Ellie that she wanted her to come and stay with her and she would let her play with her doll, Ellie thought she must be dreaming.

Now it was time for bed. The girls made a visit to the outhouse, washed their hands and faces, brushed their teeth, took a drink of water, and went up to bed. Ellie thought she had never seen a nightgown as pretty as the one her friend had. It was white with tiny red hearts and lace around the neckline and sleeves. *Everything she has is so pretty*, thought Ellie. *I wonder why she even bothers with me.*

Soon the girls were laughing and giggling about the lumpy straw tick. Missy usually slept on a firm mattress, so this was all new to her. Ellie told Missy what a time her mother and she had the last time they filled the ticks. They giggled some more when they thought about the baby who crawled inside the straw tick.

"I have never slept two in a bed," said Ellie.

"Me, either," was Missy's reply, "but I know a song about ten in a bed."

"Ten!" exclaimed Ellie.

Missy began to tell her how the song went: "There were ten in the bed and the little one said, 'Move over, move over.' So they all moved over and one fell out. There were nine in the bed and the little one said, 'Move over, move over.' So they all moved over and one fell out. There were eight in the bed ... " and so on until only one was left.

Ellie thought it was so funny. "Let's play it," she said.

So they started all over. They bounced and turned

each time they said, "Move over." But when they were down to four and went to move over, they both fell out of bed. They laughed so hard their tummies hurt.

Then Ellie heard her father call, "Ellie, you girls settle down or I'll come up there."

Quickly and as quietly as they could, they crawled back into bed. They pulled the covers up over their heads, whispered little girl secrets, and laughed their little girl giggles way into the night. Oh, this was a night they would always remember. But in spite of all the fun they were having, their eyes began to close, and before long they were peacefully asleep.

8
Forbidden Fruit

It was Sunday morning again, and the family was on its way to church. Ellie was thinking of the fun she had when Missy spent the night with her.

"Mama," she asked from her place in the front buggy box, "don't you think Missy is pretty?"

Before her mother could answer, Papa said, "Pretty is as pretty does, and what good is a pretty dish if it's empty?" Ellie did not know what he meant by those remarks, but she could tell by his tone of voice and expression that he didn't approve of her friend Missy. So she said no more. She would wait until after Sunday service, then she could relate all her recent happenings to Rachel and Alta. They were her little Amish friends, whom she saw only at church now since they moved so far away.

Papa had sold Dixie for a good price and bought a safer buggy horse. This one could run at a fair speed, too, but was much more gentle. Mother liked Molly the minute she saw her, and it was good to know that she could drive her if necessary.

Molly trotted along at an even gait, and soon they were turning in the drive of the Hershberger homestead. The Amish do not have church houses, but rather hold services in their homes. Each family takes its turn.

Jake stopped his horse by the front gate behind other buggies and waited for the womenfolk (as he called them) and the babies to alight. Then he and the boys drove toward the barn, unhitched Molly, tied her in line with the other horses, gave her a few tufts of hay, and then joined the other men and boys.

Lydia Miller took the twin Ellie had and carried her to the house. "You just bring the *Vindel Satchely* (diaper bag)," she told Ellie. "I'll take care of this little one." They went to the enclosed porch where they removed their bonnets, shawls, and capes. They laid them on a table reserved for that purpose, then joined the other women in the house. Most of the mothers with children sat in the kitchen or bedroom. The older women, young girls, and men occupied the living room and dining area, if there was a dining room available.

Now the singing began. The second song was always the same. It was *"Das Lob Lied,"* a song of praise. They sang very slowly. To sing four verses took nineteen minutes. Even before the singing was completed, Ellie's back began to ache. The benches they sat on were backless, made of hard wood, and very uncomfortable. But Ellie knew she must try to sit as still as she possibly could.

The ministers had gone to an upstairs room where chairs had been set up for them. They needed time together to discuss matters of the church, to decide in what order they would give their sermons, and to pray together. There were always three ministers, and often more, if any visiting ministers were present. The first minister would lead the opening service and read the Scripture and prayer. Then a minister, in turn, gave the main sermon. This was followed by more prayer. After that, the deacon would say a few words regarding what had been presented, and they would have another prayer. At last, after the preaching, one of the ministers would announce at whose home services were to be the next time. They held preaching service only every two weeks. The Sunday when no church was in session was known as "in-between" Sunday.

Ellie sat quietly as long as she could. She knew her mother didn't like for her to *rutsch* (stir) during church. She had forced herself to sit still all during the singing. Now the ministers had come down from upstairs, and the first one stood by the doorway between the living room and bedroom. He cleared his throat several times and, in singsong fashion, began to speak in a different German dialect than the people spoke at home every day. Ellie understood very little of what was said. Her back ached worse than ever. Her feet didn't quite touch the floor, so a spot behind her knees hurt, too. She could stand it no longer. Ellie *rutsched.* Her mother reached down and pinched her. That hurt, too, and she almost said, "Ouch!" aloud, but she caught herself in time. Well, at least she had changed position.

After the reading of Scripture and prayer, everyone stood for a short while as the minister spoke a few more words. As they were seated, the bishop arose. Ellie liked him. He was a kindly person, but spoke firmly. Often he spoke in words the children could understand and referred to Jesus' love for little ones. Time seemed to go faster when the bishop preached.

Now the lady of the house entered the room with a big bowl of homemade sugar cookies and soda crackers for the smaller children, so they wouldn't get too hungry before services were over. Ellie's mouth began to water, and she wished she were still considered young enough to take some. Then an idea popped into her head. She reached for the twin Lydia Miller had been holding all this while and sat her firmly on her own lap, turning her away from the watchful eye of her mother. Now when the cookie and cracker bowl was passed, Ellie dutifully reached in and took one of each—for the baby, of course. Some of the ladies smiled, probably thinking how considerate and kind Ellie was to take the responsibility of helping with her sisters. If they only knew!

Bending her head low, with her face very close to the baby's face, Ellie began to feed her the cookie. Every so often, a crumb would happen to break off and find its way inconspicuously into Ellie's mouth. She felt rather wicked, but oh did those crumbs ever taste good! The cracker had been placed into the twin's hand to eat by herself. Ellie knew a cracker would be too crunchy to try to eat without being caught. She also knew that even though the taste of the cookie had made her thirsty, she dare not take a drink of water which was later offered to those small children who had eaten a snack.

Now the bishop was talking about a woman who had disobeyed God by eating forbidden fruity. *Oh, my,* thought Ellie, *how can he know what I did so soon? He must have seen me.* Her head bent lower and lower, and her face burned. She was so ashamed. *Why do I do such silly, impulsive things?* she wondered. If only he hadn't seen her. Better still, if only she hadn't eaten any of the cookie.

Then she heard bishop say, "God asked Eve, 'Why did you eat of the fruit of the tree I had told you not to eat of?'" Ellie knew he was not talking about the cookie crumbs.

From that time until the last hymn was sung, Ellie listened very carefully. The baby had fallen asleep in her arms. Although she ached from holding her, Ellie bore it as patiently as she could. Perhaps this was her penance for what she had done earlier.

At five after twelve, the deacon arose and spoke once more about the message for the day. Then he announced that in two weeks church services were to be held at the Abraham Hostetler home, if the Lord willed it so.

After everyone was dismissed, the men began to push benches together to form tables. The lady of the house, her daughters, and the young teenage girls covered the benches with tablecloths and began to set food, silverware, and glasses in place. The meal consisted of homemade bean soup, bread, butter, apple butter, pickled red beets, pickles, peanut butter spread, and coffee. Everything except the coffee and peanut butter was homegrown or homemade. It looked absolutely delicious. After they all bowed their heads in silent prayer, the eating and visiting began. What a happy fellowship it was.

One of the older women again offered to help with the twins, freeing Ellie to be with her friends, whom she seldom saw anymore. After they had finished eating, three little girls found their way out to Jake Maust's buggy and sat in it to talk and share secrets.

"Something happened at our house yesterday," said Rachel. "But you can't guess."

"Tell us," begged the other two.

"Our roan cow had a baby calf."

"Well, we had a dozen chickens hatch," remarked Alta, "and they are so cute. I helped Mom take them out of the basket and we put them in the grass. Right away they started pecking for something to eat."

Now it was Ellie's turn. Not to be outdone, she began to tell them how her English girlfriend from school had spent the night with her, and what fun they had. At first, Rachel and Alta listened awestruck, and Ellie felt very important. Then it happened.

"Oh, Ellie," said Rachel, "you are making that up. My dad would never allow an Englisher to stay at our house just for fun, and I don't believe yours would either."

"Well, my papa did," answered Ellie.

"That's another thing," remarked Alta. "You are getting so 'high' since you moved and go to the outsider's school. You're even starting to talk like the English people do. My mom said she won't be surprised if a lot of their ways rub off on your family."

"My dad said that, too," Rachel exclaimed. "He said your dad is getting pretty foxy, driving fast horses and a shiny buggy."

How could they turn on me so quickly? Ellie wondered. Rachel leaned over and whispered to Alta, and then the two girls jumped out of the buggy and ran to the house, leaving a very sad and disappointed Ellie sitting all alone. Big tears began to roll down her cheeks. But she couldn't stay there forever. At last she, too, made her way to the house.

At the edge of the porch the bishop stopped her. Reaching into his inside coat pocket, he handed Ellie a piece of wintergreen candy. "I noticed how well you listened today to the preaching," he said, "so I think you can have one piece of candy, at least."

Ellie took it and barely whispered, *"Danki,"* or "thanks."

"What's the matter? Has the cat got your tongue?" asked her preacher friend.

But Ellie just shook her head and continued to the house. Not only did her back still ache, but so did her heart. Her two friends were shunning her, and now the kind bishop had given her a compliment she felt she didn't deserve. She hoped her parents were

ready to go home. That was one wish granted because, as she came into the house, her mother asked,
"Where were you? We are ready to go home, and I've
been looking all over. Hurry, now, and get the
Satchely and your wraps. You know your father
doesn't like to be kept waiting."

Ellie didn't answer, but did as she was told. When
she went to the porch to get her wraps, she saw
Rachel and Alta looking around the corner from the
kitchen door and laughing and whispering. They
looked directly at her.

Then Alta said, loud enough for others to hear,
"Ellie's going high." She knew Alta meant she was
becoming worldly like the English people.

Ellie turned and, yielding to temptation, stuck out
her tongue. And it felt good. She fled to the waiting
buggy and soon was on her way home. Tomorrow
would be another day, and surely it must be better
than today. Wait until she saw Missy. Everything
would be alright.

9
Face Cream, Perfume, and Body Powder

The strawberries were ripening and the peas needed picking. Mrs. Maust had a large garden, and canning time meant extra work. The twins were crankier than usual. They were cutting new teeth. Mounds of diapers and other clothes needed washing. How would Ellie's mother ever get everything done? She must speak to Papa again about getting an older girl to help during the summer.

After church that Sunday evening, the whole family went outdoors. While the children looked for different stones in the grass, their parents relaxed on the porch swing.

The swing was only for Sunday afternoon or evening use, since during the week work lasted from before sunup until after dark.

"Jake," Mrs. Maust began rather timidly, "do you suppose I could have some help for the summer?" She waited for his answer.

Jake cleared his throat. "You have Ellie," he remarked.

"But Ellie can't do yet what a grown girl could. She is a big help, but what with canning and the summer sewing . . . well, I just don't see how we can do it all."

Papa didn't answer for a while. Finally he said, "If you really feel you need a *Maut*, I guess we will get one."

Mrs. Maust smiled. She knew just who she would ask. Cristy Glick had a girl, Susie, who she had heard was a very good worker. She was only eighteen, so she wasn't liable to be getting married right away. Then, too, coming this far from the main Amish settlement, she wouldn't do as much *Rum-schpringe* (running around) so much in the evenings. That way, she would be just as spry and ready to work on Monday, as any other day.

But Mrs. Maust didn't really know Susie Glick very well. She put a letter in the mail first thing Monday morning and eagerly waited all week for an answer. It came in the mail on Saturday. If Lizzie Maust could make-do for two weeks yet, Susie wrote, she could work for her all summer. No one else had asked for her until two days after she got Mrs. Maust's letter.

How glad Lizzie was she had written right away on Monday. Susie had some sewing to do for herself yet before she was ready, but Lizzie would manage somehow until then. The next two weeks were two of the most hectic she had ever spent in her life. Early garden things were ready. The twins came down with old-fashioned measles. Ellie caught her arm in the washing machine wringer. The boys helped around the house as best they could, but Jake needed them in the hayfields, too.

No one knew yet except Lizzie, but by fall there would be an addition to the family. So, many days, Mother didn't feel at her best.

Finally, the two weeks had passed, and early one morning Susie arrived at the Maust home ready for work.

"Ellie, show Susie where she can put her things," Mom said. "I hope you don't mind sharing a room with Ellie."

"Yeah, what else is new?" answered Susie.

"What?" asked Lizzie. But Susie didn't say anything else—just picked up her suitcases and walked toward the stairway. She really meant that it was nothing new for her to share a room with little girls whenever she worked "out," as she called it. However, Ellie thought she had a strange way of answering her mother.

Without saying a word, Ellie led the way up to her room and opened the door. This was one of the plainest rooms Susie had ever seen. There was a closet where she could hang her good dresses at one end, a small chest of drawers, of which she could have two, and a bed.

"Not even a mirror!" exclaimed Susie. "And where is the nightstand for the lamp? I need a place to put my cream and perfume and other personal things. Don't you even have a mirror in here?" she asked in exasperation, turning to Ellie.

The shy little girl was overcome by such an unexpected outburst. She just shook her head. And why did this girl want to keep cream upstairs? Mama kept that in a crock in the basement. Ellie thought Susie was beautiful, with her dark wavy hair and rosy cheeks. She dressed pretty, too—not so drab as her own clothes were. Today she was wearing a light tan dress with sleeves that were slightly puffy and elastic around the waistband. *She looks pretty*, thought Ellie, *but she sure talks funny.*

"Well," said Susie, "I'll fix things this evening. Guess I'd better go down and get started." With that, she hung her Sunday dresses in the closet and put her suitcases down beside the chest of drawers, heading downstairs with Ellie in tow. She had a lot to learn about where everything was kept and how Mrs. Maust wanted things done, but she was a quick and willing learner and not afraid of hard work.

From the very first day, Susie could tell that Mr. Maust did not approve of her dress or the way she wore her hair. Susie didn't care. She seemed to enjoy antagonizing him further. She did little things like pushing her covering back to show more of her wavy black hair, leaving her covering strings untied, and rolling her dress sleeves above her elbows. Papa grumbled under his breath about these things and the fact that he had to pay her more than she was worth, but he couldn't honestly deny she sure was a hard worker.

Ellie soon discovered the cream Susie talked about when she first came was a face cream, which the young *Maut* used every night before retiring. It was meant to keep her skin soft and beautiful. It stood with her bottles of perfume and body powder on top of the chest of drawers. Susie always looked so pretty and smelled so good. Ellie thought about how she would like to wear perfume and use those other wonderful things.

There were only two days of school left, and Ellie hurried with the dishes. She was careless, or *doppich*, and spilled some grease drippings on the front of her apron.

"Ach, Ellie, look now, once, how you *schussel* (hurry) so. Run upstairs *schnell* (quickly) and change your apron," ordered her mother. Ellie did as she was told, but as she entered the room, her attention was drawn to the array of bottles and jars on the chest. She changed her apron, and then, though she didn't really mean to, she found herself opening a pretty bottle of perfume. It smelled so good. She put some on her dress and then, opening the jar of face cream, she quickly daubed some on her face. But she didn't have time to rub it into her skin as she had seen Susie do.

Next, she took some body powder and gave her neck a coating of that. Now she heard her mother call, so, feet flying, she ran downstairs. *Wait till my friend Missy sees me,* she thought.

Mr. Maust walked into the kitchen just as his daughter came from upstairs. He was going into Hatfield for some parts for one of his farm implements and came in for the list of things his wife said she needed him to get.

"Ellie Maust," Jake boomed, "what is that stuff on

your face? Why do you smell like that? What have you done?"

Ellie just stood there, her face a white, pasty mess. In spite of the fact that the child had been into her personal belongings, Susie had to laugh at the sight before her.

"I don't think it's anything to laugh about," Jake said curtly. "Ellie, you go and clean that stuff off and come out to the woodshed, and I mean it."

Ellie began to cry.

Mrs. Maust waved the waiting schoolbus on its way. After a hard spanking, Ellie rode to school with her father. He talked to her all the way about the sin of pride, and how God made us all and called it good, and how do we think we can improve on God's own work. A meek and tear-stained little girl entered the schoolyard and sought out her special friend for comfort. What would Ellie do after school was over? It would be a long summer without Missy.

Ellie dreaded going home that evening and facing Susie. But she need not have worried. Susie was extra nice to her, even giving her a piece of gum—on the sly, of course.

"All Susie said to her was, *"Bussli* (little kitten)"*— that was her pet name for Ellie—*"Bussli,* you had better wait until you are old enough for *Rumschpringe* before you use such things." Ellie liked her real well from then on.

Mr. Maust complained to his wife that evening, "You watch that Ellie better. I wonder if we should have taken Cristy Glick's Susie to work for us. Seems they don't make her mind. She's some fancy."

10

Fancy Buggies and Beaus

School had been over with for some time, and summer was quickly passing. Countless jars of fruit, vegetables, and preserves had been put up for the winter days ahead. Now it was time to do the sewing for next school term. Mama said Ellie was growing right out of her clothes.

When Mr. Boroky, the cloth peddler, came to their house with his van loaded with various materials, Ellie wished the choice was hers to make. Oh, what pretty pinks, yellows, and reds he had! But she was almost certain that her mother would purchase the same dull browns, dark blues, and greens she always wore.

The hired girl came out to inspect his wares and decided on a pretty rose-colored material. Noticing Ellie's wistful gaze, Susie ordered a yard and a half more than she had first asked for. She also selected a bright yellow in the same amount of yardage. Pay-ing for her purchases, Susie took her colorful pieces of goods and made her way to the house as Ellie watched, almost too awed to move.

"Now then, Mrs. Maust, what can I get for you?" asked Mr. Borsky.

"Well, first I need some good denim for the menfolk of the family. And some dark blue chambray. That's good for shirts. Something that wears well and doesn't show the dirt."

"I know," said the peddler, "you Amish people are very practical and know a good buy when you see one." Thereupon he began to show his best weaves of the materials she had mentioned.

Once those were bought, she said, "Now I will have to pick out some cloth for school dresses for this girl." Lizzie pointed toward Ellie as she spoke. "If she didn't grow so fast, she could take her Sunday dresses for school, and I'd just make her two new ones for Sunday wear. But she gets so tall already."

"Yes, they grow fast," replied the peddler. "Here are some very nice pieces," he said as he took some lovely blue, pink, and lavender cloth down from a shelf.

"Oh, no," said Mama, "I want something in a darker shade." Ellie was disappointed when she saw him replace the pieces and bring out the same old dark shades.

"Mama," ventured the young girl, "couldn't I have the light blue one? I'd take real good care of it. Please?" she looked longingly at her mother.

"It's a dollar a yard less than those are," Mr.

Borsky said, pointing to the drab ones Mrs. Maust was about to buy.

"Well, you have helped real good with the work all summer. Maybe you could wear it for Sunday. But just this one—the others will have to be dark colors." It was enough. Ellie could have jumped with joy, and she probably would have, had she known what their *Maut* had planned.

After Mrs. Maust made more purchases of buttons, thread, hooks, and eyes, she and Ellie carried the bundles of cloth to the house. In the two weeks following, it seemed that Mother's sewing machine never stopped. Susie had also brought her machine from home. In the evening, when her work for the day was done, she escaped to her room upstairs and made dresses of her own. Ellie would sit and watch her sometimes when she had been sent upstairs at bedtime. She thought she never saw such beautiful dresses. Susie had finished the rose-colored one and hung it up under her white organdy cape and apron. The pink shone through so prettily. Ellie couldn't keep her eyes off it.

"Do you like that dress?" asked Susie one evening.

"Oh, yes," Ellie said. "It's the prettiest dress I've ever seen, except maybe the yellow one my friend Missy wore at school."

"How would you like to have one?"

"Me? Oh, no. I couldn't," Ellie said.

"Why not?" Susie wanted to know.

"Oh, my pop. He wouldn't let me."

"But if someone gives you something, it's different, isn't it?"

"Well, I guess. I don't know, though—but who would ever give me something so nice?" she wondered aloud.

"I would," said Susie.

"What? You . . . oh, but you can't."

"Yes, I can, and I am going to. Not just one, but two. A rose one and a yellow one. That's why I bought more material than I needed. I'll finish my yellow one. Then I'll begin on yours."

Ellie was speechless. She wondered if her mother knew about this. And what would Papa say? Sleep wouldn't come for a long time that night. When it finally did, she dreamed she was floating on pink and yellow clouds with Papa and Mama running along, trying to pull her down. Then she sailed away, with Susie holding her hand, into a rose-colored sunset that was lined with yellow gold.

Even though the Mausts lived outside of the Amish settlement, Susie did not lack for a way to go to the young folks' gatherings. Every Sunday evening some young boy in a shiny buggy—fancied up with foxtails and battery lights—came to take Susie to the singing, and brought her home again. Mr. Maust frowned on so much running around, and also at the fancy buggies and boys that invaded his property every week.

He knew Susie would be hard to replace as a worker, so he put up with some things of which he didn't approve. Still, he had made up his mind that as soon as the summer work was over and the new baby was there, Susie must go.

Sunday night came again. After chores, Ellie saw

Susie run upstairs to get ready for the singing. She followed her.

"Come in, Bussli," Susie invited. Ellie sat on the bed and watched Susie slip into her rose-colored dress.

"Where are you going?" asked Ellie.

"My beau and I are going to the singing."

"What's a beau?" asked Ellie.

"Why, my boyfriend."

"Will I ever have a beau?" Ellie wanted to know.

"Oh, sure, you will, a girl as pretty as you. You will have lots of beaus."

"And can I ride in a fancy buggy?"

"Of course, in the fanciest."

"Oh, my!" said Ellie. She felt warm all over.

Soon they heard the sound of a buggy coming down the drive. Susie hurried downstairs and out to the buggy, just as it pulled up to the gate. *She looks like a picture*, thought Ellie, turning as Susie waved.

"See you in the morning, Bussli," she called.

I'll be glad when it's me that is riding in a fine buggy with my beau, Ellie mused. Then she heard Mother call, and she came back to reality once more. Should she tell Mother about the present Susie was making for her? No, she decided to wait and let Susie tell her. But all evening she kept thinking of pretty dresses, fancy buggies, and beaus.

Next to Missy, she had another close friend. She hoped Susie would stay with them forever.

11
As the Twig
Is Bent

A new baby joined the Maust family in late September—another boy. This one they named Andy. The hired girl had consented to stay and help out until Mrs. Maust was able to carry on the household duties. Ellie was glad Susie was staying longer. She was also happy that school would soon begin and she could see her little English friend each day again. There was so much to tell her—all about her new baby brother, the *Maut*, her pet lamb, Susie's many beaus, but especially the pretty dresses which were given to her by her good friend, Susie.

Oh, and about those dresses. Ellie would never forget the evenings spent in the making and trying on of those two garments.

"When are you going to tell Mama?" Ellie inquired one evening as they were doing a fitting.

"Hush, Bussli, and hold still. How can I finish if you wiggle so? Once we get the dresses done, we will show your mother. If I tell her now, she is liable to talk to your papa about it, and he might just get a notion I can't make them for you. But once they are finished, he may let you wear them. For who else would they fit?"

What wisdom this young lady has, thought Ellie.

"Besides, won't your folks be surprised? Everyone likes surprises. Here, lift your arms so I can see if I need to cut out any more before attaching the sleeves. Oh, you look so pretty in pink. Yellow goes with your dark hair and eyes nicely, too. Just you wait, young lady. You will break more than one boy's heart."

She didn't really know what Susie meant, but it sounded important.

Talk about surprises! Well, when the dresses were completed, Susie was in for the surprise.

"Come and put on your rose dress now, and we will go down and show your folks how nice you look. I'll bring the yellow one." Ellie slipped into her new dress and apron. "Oh, you look so cute. Wait until they see."

Slowly the girls descended the stairs and made their appearance in the living room, where Papa was reading and Mother was feeding the baby. Mrs. Maust let out a gasp, which caused Jake to look up from the paper in his hand.

"Ach, my," was all Mama said. But Mr. Maust said plenty. The joy all left Ellie's face and her eyes lost their sparkle as she heard her papa say, "Ellie, you go right upstairs and get out of that outlandish dress." Then he rebuked his wife for allowing their daughter to dress in such a worldly fashion.

"Such bright colors," he said. "Lizzie, you know it's forbidden. If we let her wear clothes like this now and go against the rules of the church, what will she be like when she grows up? As the twig is bent, so grows the tree. From now on, when the dry goods van comes here, I'll do the buying. That light blue material that she wore last Sunday is plenty fancy. I never thought you'd go so far as to buy such loud colors."

Mrs. Maust was too stunned to answer, but the hired girl wasn't. Never had she spoken up to her employer before, but this was too much. "Jake," she ventured, "your wife didn't buy the goods for these dresses, nor did she make them. In fact, she didn't know any more about it than you did until now. If there is any blame, I'll take it all. When I bought the materials for my own dresses, I saw how wistfully Ellie looked at them and—"

"Huh!" interrupted Jake. "Wistfully? The lust of the eye is what I'd call it."

Susie continued, "Ellie is such a hard worker and a good girl, so—"

"Yes, and I aim to keep her that way," Mr. Maust said, once again breaking into Susie's speech.

"Well, she isn't a member of the church yet, and I know she needs more school clothes. Surely she could wear them for school. I just wanted to give her a gift," remarked Susie.

Mrs. Maust was appalled at the *Maut's* spunk.

"Are you finished?" thundered Jake. "We can clothe our own children. If you wanted to give her a gift, you could have given her a nice dish or something fit for our people. Now go upstairs like I told you, Ellie, and change your dress."

"You are impossible!" was all Susie said, as she and Ellie turned and went back upstairs.

Ellie began to cry. *Now,* she thought, *I'll never get to wear my beautiful dresses.*

"Don't cry, Bussli," Susie said. "I'll talk to your mom. She isn't as strict as your papa is. Maybe we can work something out yet. Come, now. I'll help you get undressed." And then she hung the dresses neatly in the closet, where Ellie feared they must stay forever.

"I know what," remarked Susie a few days later. "Every night when we come upstairs to get ready for bed, Ellie, you will put on one of your new dresses for me and pretend we are in school. I will act as if I were your very good friend. You know, the one you told me about."

"Oh, you mean Missy?"

"Yes, that's the one. Missy, what a different name. Well, anyway, we will play school, and you will have the prettiest dress of all."

"Susie," Ellie exclaimed, "I like you so much! Can't you stay here all the time?"

"No, I'm afraid not. You see, I promised my own mother I'd help her a while, and then—now this is a secret I haven't told anyone—I plan to get married in the spring. I know you won't tell, that's why I'm telling you. Besides, we are special friends."

"Married!" exclaimed Ellie. "Oh, Susie, who are you marrying?"

"It's the boy who came to see me more than any other. The one with the high-steppin' horse and—"

"And the fancy buggy," interrupted Ellie.

"Yes, that's the one. He only asked me last Sunday night after the singing."

"But you and he aren't even baptized yet, and Papa says he is worldly."

"Don't tell anyone this, either, but we plan to join another church. We know we wouldn't be satisfied staying with the Old Order."

Now many thoughts raced through Ellie's mind. Was Susie wicked? How could she be, when she was so nice to her?

The two weeks that followed flew by, it seemed. Susie could not persuade Lizzie Maust to let Ellie wear her yellow or rose dress to school. Being a good and faithful wife, she stood by her husband, even at times when he seemed extra strict.

Ellie thought she couldn't stand it when the time came for the *Maut* to leave. She watched Susie pack her clothes and various other items.

"Want to help?" asked Susie. "Hand me my cold cream jar, and the perfume bottles." She put them carefully between clothes, so the jars and bottles wouldn't break. "Now, I'll take the powder." Then, noticing how longingly Ellie looked at the box of body powder, she handed it back and said, "No, you take it. Just don't use too much, or your papa will find out."

"Me?" asked Ellie, astonished at the thought.

"Why not?" commented Susie. "What's wrong with smelling good?"

"Well, maybe I'll keep it till I'm old enough for *Rum-schpringe,* then I'll use it."

"You do that!" laughed Susie.

Mrs. Maust called upstairs, "Susie, are you about ready? Jake is waiting." Mr. Maust was going to town this Saturday to pick up some things he needed, and also a few groceries. So it had been decided that he would take the *Maut* home. He was the only member of the Maust family that was glad to see her go.

Ellie stood by the buggy as Susie loaded her suitcases and then climbed in and sat next to Jake. One thing was sure, neither Jake nor Susie relished this trip together. Mr. Maust took up the lines and, without a word, slapped the horse across the back with his whip. They took off with a jerk. Susie looked back and called, "Good-bye, Bussli, be good," and they were gone.

Mr. Maust looked straight ahead and spoke not a word as they rode all twelve miles. Once they reached the Glick homestead, he asked, "Well, what do I owe you?" Because of his dislike for Susie and her disrespect for him, she made her price a little higher than usual. Yet she felt she really had earned every penny of it. Jake mumbled as he reached for his checkbook. Mrs. Glick came out the front door.

"Well, hello, Susie. You're home. Here, I'll help you with the suitcases. How's your wife and baby doing, Jake?"

He mumbled his answer, handed Susie her check, and said he had to be on his way. But after he left, he thought to himself. *If that Susie were my girl, she would have learned more respect a long time ago. And her own mother acted as if she didn't care how spiffy she looked today when she came home. Well, whose fault is it? I say if the parents don't bend the twig to go straight, all they get is a crooked tree.* But Susie didn't care what Jake thought. Though she would miss her little Bussli, it was good to be home again.

12

Too Smart Yet

The hours seemed so empty to Ellie, now that Susie was gone. At night there was no one to talk with or snuggle up to during the thunderstorms she dreaded so much. Several days after the hired girl left, Ellie went upstairs to go to bed and, opening the closet door, discovered her beautiful dresses were gone. Just to look at them and feel the smoothness of the material had brought some comfort, but no more. It seemed everything was taken from her. Ellie climbed into bed and cried herself to sleep. In the days that followed, she wondered if she might ask her mother what happened to those dresses, but she never did.

One day at school, Missy begged her to come spend a night at her house.

"You owe me a visit," she said. "It's been a long time since we spent the night together. Please come," pleaded Missy.

"But I must ask my mother first, and she will have to ask Papa. That's how they always do," answered Ellie.

"Oh, ask tonight, please. You will, won't you? Oh, I hope you can come. I told my mama I was going to invite you, and she thought that would be so nice. Then I'll show you my doll collection and my music boxes. We will have a lot of fun. I can't wait until tomorrow. I just know your parents will say yes!"

But Ellie wasn't so sure. She almost dreaded going home that night and hearing what the answer might be. Why, oh why, did she have to be Amish?

As she stepped inside the kitchen, the smell of freshly baked bread and rolls greeted her. The canary was singing in its cage by the window, and the twins came running, glad she was home. Home, she thought. Maybe it's not such a bad place after all.

"Hurry and change your dress, Ellie," her mother instructed. "We have a lot to do yet tonight. I didn't get the ironing done, and we need to pick the last of the lima beans. But fill the oil lamps first so that's done before dark. You can iron, then, until chore time, and we will pick the limas after supper. The twins can do the dishes—they are old enough now to help, too."

Ellie was glad that the twins were older and could help with small chores now. But as she grew, she was taught to do more grown-up tasks, such as ironing, washing, baking, and more of the cleaning and garden work. She was busier than ever.

Lizzie saw her daughter eyeing the fresh rolls. "Ach," she said, "I guess you are hungry. Take one roll and eat it quick, Bussli. Now look what that Susie has done! She mixed me up so with your name. Go on now, Ellie. Here come the boys, and they will want something to eat, too."

Ellie quickly took a sweet roll and ate it on the way upstairs to change her dress. But Mother had called her "Bussli!" It sounded good again, even if it was not done intentionally.

Back in the kitchen, Ellie cleaned all the lunch pails, put them on the shelf, and set up the ironing board. The flatirons had to be heated on the woodstove. They were heavy for her young arms to handle, but she worked diligently. She wanted to please her mother.

The weather was still warm outside, and the heat from the stove made the kitchen very hot indeed. Every once in a while, a wisp of a dark curl stuck to her forehead. She brushed it back away from her face and went right on ironing. All the while, Ellie kept wondering when to ask if she could spend the next night with her friend.

After supper, while they were picking beans, Ellie found the courage to approach her mother with the request that had been on her mind all day.

"Ellie, Ellie, why must you come up with such ideas? You know I will need to ask Papa."

"Missy asked me to come. She said her mother thinks it would be nice, so I know it's alright with her."

"Well, you helped real good all summer with the work. Now that we won't be so busy anymore until butchering time, maybe we could spare you for one night ... if you get up in the morning early enough to fill the reservoir and help me make the half-moon pies and a few extra things." Noticing the pleased look on her daughter's face, Mrs. Maust quickly added, "Don't get your hopes up, now; mind, we don't know what Papa will say."

Well, Papa said plenty. Mother approached him after the day's work was done. Ellie didn't hurry upstairs as she generally did.

"What are you waiting for?" Jake asked as he glanced up from his paper and saw Ellie standing by the hickory rocker. "Well, speak up. Are you going to tell me or just stand there?"

Ellie began to tremble. "I—well, Missy—remember once...." She couldn't go on. Lizzie took pity on her stammering daughter and came to her aid.

"Jake, the little crippled girl who spent the night here with Ellie a long time ago wants her to go along to her house and return the visit. Her mother said it would be nice."

"Nice? Nice for whom?" asked Jake. "Lizzie, you know you need Ellie here. She picked up enough worldly ideas when that Susie Glick was here. We need not send her out to the home of an Englisher to see more. In a few years, I'm keeping her out of school altogether. All this book learning makes her too smart yet. First thing, she will want to know more than her parents. You go on to bed, Ellie, and get this nonsense out of your head."

Mrs. Maust saw the terror in Ellie's face at the mention of removing her from school. Ellie was afraid of losing one more thing that was especially dear to her. She could hardly bear it. How could she ever get along without Missy?

Mrs. Maust followed her daughter upstairs. "Don't cry, Bussli," she said. This time she called her that on purpose. She wiped her daughter's face and told her tenderly, "Go to bed. Papa didn't say no yet. Give me some more time to talk with him. Maybe he doesn't understand."

"No, Mama, he doesn't understand. I don't want to be smarter than you or Papa. Really, I don't. I just want to visit my very best friend, and I do want to be a good girl."

"I know you do. Just try to sleep. You may feel better in the morning."

Ellie lay awake for a long time wondering how soon she must quit school. First the *Maut* left, and now she might have to part with Missy.

Ellie never knew what her mother said to Papa, but the next morning Mama told her she could stay the night with her dear friend.

"Do your work well and quickly. And don't say anything to upset your father. He means well, Ellie. You may think he is too strict, but he only wants you to grow up to be a good Amish girl and obey."

"And not get too smart yet," the girl remembered.

"That, too," answered Lizzie.

It would take a long time to tell of all Ellie and Missy did and saw that day and night. But Ellie felt as if she were flying as she told her friend the good news. They didn't have to do any work at Missy's house. All they did was play. Never had Ellie seen such a grand place. When you wanted lights to see by, all you needed to do was push a button. Water came from pipes by the kitchen sink, and the bathroom was just like the one at school. Ellie walked around in a daze. But when she saw Missy's dolls and her music boxes, she was speechless.

She enjoyed every minute, and in her heart she knew she would never forget this day. Forever she would be grateful to her parents for permitting her this visit. Forever!

13

The Big Sale

"Oh, Mama, you should have seen Missy's house, and all her clothes and dolls. She had dolls with hair you could comb and eyes that opened and closed. And music boxes, too. The prettiest one had a girl standing on one foot. She wore a little pink dress. When Missy turned a key, the girl went round and round." Ellie was bubbling with joy. "Thank you for letting me go."

"Hush, Ellie," said Lizzie. "Don't say anything like this that Papa can hear. He is afraid you will want things like that—things that are not for us plain people. See how glad the twins are to have you home again, and so am I. And look how the baby is reaching out for you to take him. Ellie, would you trade little Andy for all the dolls Missy has, or for her pretty music boxes?"

Ellie hadn't thought of it that way at all. But without hesitating, she quickly answered, "Never."

Contrary to what some might believe, Mr. Maust was a good husband and father. Yes, he did expect obedience and that his children learn to work. And he taught them right from wrong. He would bring them treats from the country store and often told them stories of when he was a little boy. His children cherished such times. They especially enjoyed the big rope swing he had made for them by the big cottonwood tree in the far corner of their backyard. Sometimes he pushed them high into the air; but he was a busy man, and such occasions were rare.

Roy and Sammie were old enough now to be trusted alone with the workhorses to plow and work the fields. Jake mentioned something several times about needing more land. So it was no surprise to his wife when he came home from town one day with the news that he heard Amos Schrock had his place up for sale, and he planned to go see Amos about buying.

"Are you sure we can handle such a big farm?" questioned Mrs. Maust.

"The boys are old enough now. They need more to do," Jake said. "And Ellie is about grown. I want to get back to the settlement before they start going with the young folks here. We made good at this place. I figure by selling the place and livestock, plus some implements, we should have a good amount to pay on the Schrock homestead. I'll keep a few cows and soon build up a good herd again.

Lizzie thought for a moment. "I will need some help to get ready to move and settle into a big house like Amos's havo," she said. "So we have to get a *Maut* again."

"I'll get you a *Maut*, if you need one," Jake replied, "but I guarantee you it won't be Susie Glick." Lizzie just smiled.

The next six weeks were busy ones. Mr. Maust had no problem selling his place, because of the improvements he and his wife had made since moving there. He received even more than he expected he could get. Also, Amos Schrock felt he could come down in price for his farm, since he was selling to a fellow church member. They were glad to see him move his family back into the Amish settlement again.

The *Maut* that came to help was no Susie Glick, in more ways than one. She was not happy and jolly like Susie, nor did she work as well, and she most certainly was not kind to Ellie. But she dressed very plain, so Papa was satisfied.

All the good dishes had been packed into boxes and neatly stacked in the corner of Ellie's and the hired girl's room. The walls and ceilings were washed, the basement cleaned, the empty jars taken from their rack and carefully wrapped to prevent breakage.

The night before the Saturday of the big sale day, Papa and the boys lined up things outside. It was all so exciting. Ellie couldn't settle down to sleep that night. It was late when she went to bed.

"Stop your *rutsching* (squirming) and go to sleep," said Mattie Yoder, their new hired girl. Ellie tried harder than ever to lie still. She ached all over. Her leg cramped, then her back itched. Finally, she could stand it no longer. She moved. A poke in the ribs from Mattie's elbow caused her to cry out.

"Ouch!" she exclaimed.

"Get out," scolded the *Maut*. "If you can't hold still, then sleep on the floor. This bed isn't big enough for both of us, anyway."

True, thought Ellie. *It would take a big bed just for you alone. You are so fat.* Without saying a word, Ellie took her pillow and curled up on the floor. She was cold all night and couldn't help but think how understanding Susie would be if she were here. Even now, she could hear her in her thoughts, saying, *What's wrong, Bussli? Can't you sleep? I know you hate to leave your friend at school, but there will be other friends. I'm here, so try to sleep. Tomorrow things will look brighter.* Oh, how she missed Susie.

Early next morning, people began to come from all directions for the Maust auction. There were more cars there than horses and buggies. Mrs. Maust had decided to sell a few household items, and among them was the small chest of drawers in Ellie's room. After breakfast, she sent Mattie up with a box to empty it of its contents. Then she had Roy and Sammie carry it down and set it in the yard along with the other things to be sold. A few minutes later Ellie heard the hired girl come downstairs.

Calling to Mrs. Maust, Mattie said for all to hear, "Look what I found in your daughter's chest of drawers," and she held out the box of body powder Susie had given Ellie.

Ellie felt cold all over. She had forgotten to hide

the powder when she knew that piece of furniture was to be sold.

"Throw it in the trash," Lizzie instructed. Mattie smirked at Ellie as she marched out the back door to the trash barrel, where she deposited the box and its contents with a plop.

You wait, reasoned Ellie. *You won't get away with this. When you aren't around, I'll go and get it back.*

The care of baby Andy had been assigned to Ellie for the day. Many people stopped to fuss over the "cute little fellow," as they called him. This embarrassed Ellie. She said very little to anyone until she saw Missy and her father coming up the walk toward the house. Ellie was surprised and delighted to see her good friend here today.

"Come in, Missy. You can stay with me. I have to take care of the baby."

"Can I hold him?" asked Missy.

"I don't care. If you want to, you can," she answered. Rather reluctantly, the baby sat on the Englisher's lap. He kept looking at her with big somber eyes and a solemn expression.

"Well, I'll come for you when I'm ready to go," said Missy's father. "Don't be a bother, now."

Ellie heard the auctioneer only when he was selling close by the house. She never knew anyone could talk so fast. Half of it she couldn't understand, and she and Missy laughed at the way he sounded.

Missy told Ellie how lucky Ellie was to have a real baby to play with, and not pretend ones like her dolls. Missy also told her she wished she could wear long dark dresses with matching aprons and a white cap, or a black one like Ellie sometimes wore. And Ellie told Missy how she wished she could always have what she asked for like Missy could, even if Mama and Papa said that spoils a child.

The sale lasted almost all day, but by evening, everyone had gone, and Papa and Mother were happy and content.

"Everything brought a good price today," Jake said. "The Lord has blessed us richly." Of course, he spoke this in German, but Ellie understood, and she was glad. Only one thing overshadowed her happiness. When they moved, it meant leaving Missy. Well, it wouldn't be for two more weeks; and to a child, two weeks can be a long time. She wouldn't worry yet. There was too much to do to worry.

14
A Hard
Good-Bye

On Monday morning following the sale, Ellie heard her father tell Roy to haul the trash barrel down to the junk pile in the orchard before leaving for school.

"Take the sorrels and hitch them to the mud boat. You can do it if you hurry."

Then Ellie remembered the box of body powder. Very quickly, on the pretense of needing to go to the outhouse, she ran out the back door. Going directly to the trash barrel, she looked inside. To her delight, she saw what she was looking for. It lay along the side of the barrel, partly hidden by other discarded bottles, tins, and various debris. Could she reach it? Ellie wondered. Well, she was sure going to try. Pulling herself up to her full height, she bent in over the top and reached down as far as she could. Her fingertips just barely touched the lid of the box. She knew she must hurry or she might be discovered in the act.

Once more she tried, and this time she got it. Some of the powder spilled, but Ellie brushed it off. Concealing her treasure inside her pocket, and using her apron to cover her dress, she returned to the house. The box left quite a bulge, so she held her arm to her side, hiding the evidence.

"Why do you walk around with your arm so close to your side?" asked the *Maut*.

But before Ellie could answer the busybody, her mother said, "Ellie, the schoolbus is here."

Gratefully, Ellie grabbed her lunch pail and ran out the door. Once she was seated, she carefully removed the box from her pocket and put it in her lunchbox. She was glad Roy and Sammie both had their noses in their schoolbooks. That way they didn't notice what she was doing. She decided to hide the powder box inside her desk until she could figure out a way to sneak it back home and to hide it from Mattie Yoder.

This was the last week Ellie and her brothers were attending Hatfield School. The teacher told Ellie she was sorry to see her go because she was such a good student and obedient child.

"Really, I can't call you a child anymore," she said. "You are a young lady, and a friend worth knowing. Your parents surely are teaching you well."

Ellie was embarrassed at such flattery but managed to say, "I'll miss you, Mrs. Kirk." Ellie liked Mrs. Kirk almost as well as she had liked Miss Olive during her first year of school.

Friday came all too soon for Ellie. She wished with all her heart she had a present to give her best friend. At noon recess, the two girls talked and planned how they might stay in touch.

"We could write to each other," said Missy, her blue eyes sparkling. "But you must write to me first so I will have your address."

"But I don't have any envelopes or stamps, and Papa wouldn't like it if I asked him for some," answered Ellie.

"Why not?" asked Missy. "My father gives me almost anything I want. Is your papa mean?"

"No, no," remarked Ellie quickly. "He just doesn't think it's necessary. I asked him once when I wanted to write to Susie Glick, and he said it would be a waste of money."

"Well, then," said Missy, "I will write to you and send an extra envelope and some stamps. That will be my going-away present to you." How Ellie wished she had a present to give to Missy.

The school bell rang, calling the boys and girls in from recess. Two of the bigger boys came running and crowded in ahead of Missy and Ellie. In so doing, they knocked Missy over. She fell on a piece of broken concrete near the first step going into the schoolhouse and cut an ugly gash in her forehead. Ellie reached down to help her to her feet. The boys ran on, not caring. But another girl ran for the teacher, and soon they were leading the injured girl to the washroom. Mrs. Kirk sent the children back to the playground so she could attend to Missy. But Ellie did not want to go back outside. Instead, she went straight to her room and sat with her head on her desk. She felt so sorry her friend was hurting.

Ellie was hurting, too—hurting because she had nothing to give her.

Reaching inside her desk for a handkerchief to dry her tears, Ellie's hand touched the powder box. She had almost forgotten it. Then a happy thought came to her. *I will give it to Missy. Susie would understand. Besides, it will be a long time before it's time for Rumschpringe,* she reasoned. Quickly she took the box and wiped it with her hanky. Tearing a sheet of paper from her writing tablet, she decorated it, drawing pretty flowers and birds and stars. On a small piece of paper she wrote, "I'll never forget you, Missy."

Wrapping the box and note with her handiwork, she glued the corners firmly with her school paste. It made a neat little package. Even though Papa would have chided her for wasting paper, crayons, and paste, she didn't feel at all guilty. Then Ellie remembered to quickly write her new address on a slip of paper, fastening it to the package for Missy so she could write.

Presently the teacher came into the room to get Missy's lunchbox and gather up a few of her other things. "Why, Ellie," she exclaimed. "Why aren't you outside playing with the other children?"

"Oh," answered Ellie, "I just made a surprise for Missy. Is she hurt bad?"

"Probably not seriously, but to be safe a doctor should check her. So Mr. Banks, the janitor, is taking her home."

"Would you please give this to her for me?" asked Ellie, handing the package to her teacher.

"Sure I will," answered Mrs. Kirk, seeing the troubled look in Ellie's eyes and hearing the anxiety in her voice. "Don't worry. Missy will be alright."

In a way, Ellie was almost glad she didn't have to say good-bye to Missy. It would have been too heartbreaking. How Ellie hoped she would soon hear from her English friend, and with the good news that she was well again.

Somehow Ellie made it through the rest of the school day. Soon she was cleaning out her desk and neatly placing all her belongings in a brown paper bag provided by Mrs. Kirk. As she left the schoolyard for the last time, she wondered if she would ever see Missy again.

"Change your dress right away," were the first words Ellie heard as she passed through the kitchen door. "We will be so busy the next week, every minute must count. Moving is a big job, and I need all the help I can get," said her mother.

Ellie hurried across the kitchen toward the stairway. At the same moment, Mattie came out of the pantry with a crock of apple butter. They collided. Mattie and the apple butter crock hit the floor with a crash. Ellie just stood there dumbfounded.

"Ach, my, what a mess," said Lizzie Maust, as she came to the aid of her *Maut*. Mattie had apple butter on her dress, apron, face, arms, and even in her hair. When she got to her feet and recovered her voice, she began scolding Ellie.

"You *doppich* little snipe. Why don't you watch where you are going? If you wouldn't always have your head so full of school and that . . . that . . . crippled little English sinner."

"But it was an accident, Mattie," said Lizzie, coming to her daughter's defense.

"Accident!" snapped Mattie. "It's about time you take that young miss in hand and teach her other things besides what she learned at that English school. I'd say it's high time you move back to our Amish community."

"I'm sorry," Ellie apologized.

"Humph," snorted Mattie. If Ellie had not been so frightened, she would have burst out laughing at the sight before her. Susie Glick would have laughed if she had collided with Ellie. *Mattie is no Susie*, Ellie thought. But Papa liked Mattie for a hired girl because she obeyed the rules of the church and wasn't fancy. Even though she was not as good a worker— yes, even though she charged more for her services—he still preferred Mattie as their *Maut*.

Ellie would find out the following week just how difficult and unreasonable Mattie could be. She almost wished she was back in the English school, even if her life there had often been unpleasant because of the fun poked at her for being Amish. But that was all in the past, and she would just make the best of whatever lay ahead.

15
Ellie's
Own Room

It was a busy week, to be sure, just as Mrs. Maust had predicted. There were hundreds of trips to the basement and just as many to the attic. By evening, Ellie was so tired, she didn't even mind Mattie's snoring.

Ellie had just come up from the basement, where her mother had sent her, when she heard Mattie say, "Well, I'll make it for her if she will listen to me."

"Oh, I'm sure you won't have any trouble. She is really a good girl. And I do think she should start wearing a cape and apron to church now. She will be thirteen next March." Ellie wondered if they were talking about her. She listened intently.

Then she heard Mattie say, "Well, if Ellie thinks I'm going to make her apron with a wide belt like some are starting to wear, she can just forget it. I'm making her the same kind of white organdy cape and apron I wear."

"Oh, that's how I want it to be. I wouldn't ask you to make it for her at all. But since you can only help until after we have moved, I figured we'd better do it now. Once I'm alone again, without a *Maut*, I likely won't get it done." Sure enough, it was Ellie they were discussing. She would feel very grown up next church Sunday.

Moving day came at last. Five of Papa's former neighbors came to help, and all five brought their wives along. Mrs. Maust was glad, for she surely needed help. The men had brought their wagons and teams of horses, while the women came together in a double buggy, or surrey, as some called them.

"I hope the men take your cookstove, table, and dishes first," said Amos's Sarah. "We need to start cooking the noon meal at your new house as soon as we can."

"Oh, I think Jake will see to that," answered Lizzie. "He likes his meals ready on time."

"So does my husband," remarked Edna Boley.

"Mine, too," Mrs. Hostetler chimed in.

"Well, then, with so many particular *Mannsleit* (menfolk), we had better make sure that goes with the first wagon load." And Mrs. Maust went to remind her husband what should be placed on the first wagon to leave.

As usual there was a lot of clean bantering and good-natured humor among the Amish all during the day. It made the workload seem lighter.

"Say, Cristy," said Yost Hostetler, "are you sure you can lift your end of those boxes, or should I get the men to help?" This he said in fun, because some

of the women had sent him to the buggy with several
boxes of food that they didn't want to send with the
wagons.

"Oh, no," Cristy answered, "if I can't make it, I'll
rest several times and eat a couple pieces of this
good pie to get my strength back, while you poor
fellows sweat it out loading the heavy stuff."

Ellie liked to hear their jolly laughter. It made her
happy to see everyone work so well together.

"Stop standing there staring, and start carrying
some of the things down from upstairs," snapped
Mattie.

Ellie jumped. She hadn't even been aware that the
Maut was nearby. But she should have known. It
seemed Mattie was everywhere, always keeping an
eagle eye on Ellie. Was it wrong to be glad that moving was almost over with, and Mattie would leave
the Maust household? Why did Mattie think she
could tell Ellie what to do, when Ellie's mother was
right there? Nevertheless, she turned and, like an
obedient girl, began to bring boxes and clothing and
other things from the upstairs.

The twins were a big help, too, and the boys
worked almost like grown men—all except the
youngest one, of course. With so many willing
hands, everything was soon ready to go. If this had
been in the days of the Old West, you would have
heard, "Wagons, ho!" Instead Mr. Maust said,
"That's it, men; let's get going," and they were on
their way.

Ellie turned for one last look. She remembered
some good times here and some not so pleasant. But

most of all she remembered Missy, her dear friend.

Now it was time to move on. *What will our new house look like?* she wondered. Not even Mama had seen it, so she couldn't ask her. Papa was more interested in the land and barn than the house, so he hadn't paid much attention, either. Mama knew only that it was a big house.

"Turn around and sit still," ordered Mattie. This time she was addressing the twins, who were riding with Ellie and the *Maut* in the buggy. Mama, the baby, and two of the other women were taking the other rig. Ellie felt sorry for her sisters. They were simply curious, as young girls naturally are. And they were also very excited. They had never known any home other than the one they were leaving. Mattie mumbled something to herself, but Ellie heard the expression, "Some people's children!" She said this in German, but Ellie understood.

Mile after mile they rode along the country roads, until finally they came to their new home. The big white house stood back from the road a way. Stately pines lined either side of the winding lane, like so many sentinels standing guard. A porch went all the way around the front of the house and part of one side, past the kitchen door. Maple trees shaded the well-kept lawn, which was hemmed in by a white picket fence.

While the girls were admiring the house, their brothers' interest was held by the large red barn and other outbuildings. They noticed a big loafing shed for cattle and the windmill that would supply water for the stock. A buggy shed that would easily house four buggies caught their eyes. Then there was the tool shop, the granary, the corncribs, and two big silos. They knew this would mean a lot of work. But for such young robust fellows, it was a challenge.

When the buggy stopped, Ellie and her sisters jumped to the ground and ran for the house.

"Here! Come back right now," they heard Mattie say. But they were so excited that all three kept going—into the kitchen, then into another large room, and on into another even larger room. One of the twins spied the door leading upstairs. Each one made a dash for the stairway, anxious to explore every inch of the new house.

"Oh, so many rooms!" exclaimed Annie.

"Yes," answered Ellie, "and I know which one I want already."

"Every room has a closet in it, too," remarked Fannie. They all agreed it was nicer than they had over imagined.

"We had better go back downstairs and help carry things in," said Ellie.

"Mama, I want the room above the living room. Can I have it?" asked Ellie expectantly.

"Well, you might want it, but I know what you'd get if I had it to say," Mattie broke in. Ellie hadn't seen her coming in when she had made her request.

"We will see," was all Mrs. Maust said. Right now she had more pressing decisions to make.

First of all, the stove was brought in and set in place. A fire was started right away. Next the table, dry sink, and cupboard arrived. With so many good workers, all Lizzie seemed to hear was, "Where do you want this?" or "Where does this go?" Her head seemed to be spinning, and to make matters worse, little Andy clung to her and refused to let anyone else take care of him. He couldn't understand what was going on and wanted to go home. It would be an adjustment for all of the family, but especially for young Andy.

The downstairs furniture was soon set in place. When the noon meal was over, Lizzie told the twins to wash the dishes while the hired girl and Ellie took the clothes and bedding upstairs.

"The men will set up the beds and carry up the dressers and trunks and whatever else is too heavy for the women."

The hired girl made sure she was the first one upstairs and directed the men where to put each item. Ellie's heart sank when she saw them carry her bed to the northwest room. She had so wanted the southeast one, facing the pond and the huge willow tree.

"Wait a minute," she said. "I think you have it wrong. My room is over here."

"Did anyone tell you so?" asked Mattie.

"Well, no, not exactly."

"Then we will leave it," ordered the *Maut.* Ellie could have cried.

Why, oh why, didn't Mattie like her? Had Ellie known then what was to happen later that day, she wouldn't have cared that all her things were moved into the north room. Swallowing hard to keep her emotions under control, she kept on working.

Before the girls had finished upstairs, little Andy

fell asleep. While he was napping, Mrs. Maust decided she needed to check on how everything was going, and she joined the girls.

"Oh," she exclaimed, "I thought you wanted the southeast room, Ellie!"

"I did," answered her daughter, "but Mattie said I should take this one."

"We will just have to change it, then," said Mrs. Maust. "Ellie will need more privacy now that she's older. Besides, this room is better for the twins. It has a double closet. And Roy and Sam should take the room above the kitchen. It's not as warm in the winter, I suppose, and they can stand it better than the girls. So we will just have to start switching furniture and clothes around."

Mattie's face looked red, and she mumbled to herself again, but Ellie did not even care. If she had ever appreciated her mother, she certainly did now. By evening, everything was in place, and the family settled into their new home.

16
Susie Glick
Stops In

It was sure nice for the family to be alone again once the hired girl left. Ellie had found a small framed mirror in the corner of her closet, and had carefully brought it out and set it on her dresser. She was very grateful for such a find because she was now old enough to put up her own hair, and it was hard to do it neatly without a looking glass.

Yes, she was now considered a young lady. Wearing a cape and apron and putting your hair up in a bun instead of braids were marks of growing up. Ellie was one of those fortunate girls with wavy brown hair, but sometimes it was hard to manage. No matter how she tried, there were always a few stray tresses that escaped from beneath her cap, to the annoyance of her father.

The first Sunday Ellie appeared in church wearing her new cape and apron and sat with the young girls instead of on the same bench with her mother, she knew there would be trouble. Not because she wasn't going to behave; oh, no, not that! Her father had instructed her very well concerning proper conduct.

It was her two Amish friends, Rachel and Alta. They were not quite as old as Ellie, and still dressed as children. Until they, too, could wear young ladies' garb, they were cruel to Ellie, whispering about her and poking fun. They accused her of being proud. For several Sundays, Ellie spent her time after services standing alone, looking forward to when it was time to go home.

Then a new family moved into the South Church district, and once again Ellie found a real friend. Her name was Cora, and right away the two girls were attracted to each other. They were about the same age, and both had just finished school. Now when Rachel and Alta whispered or made snide remarks, it didn't really matter. There was someone else to befriend her and to share her dreams and secrets.

"Want to come home with me after church next Sunday?" Ellie asked Cora. "I'd really like to have you."

"Oh, I don't know if I could. They need me to help chore."

"Yes, I know what that's like. I always have to help at home, too."

"Wonder, if I'd ask, if I would be allowed to come Saturday evening after chores and spend the night? Sunday morning the men could do the chores alone, since they needn't go out to do the field work."

"That would be fun. Please ask your folks," begged Ellie.

Cora asked and was granted permission to go. That was just one of many nights and days that the girls spent together at each other's homes.

Ellie learned many new tasks. Soon she was baking bread, pies, and cakes just as well as her mother could. Now she also made her own clothes, plus those of her brothers and sisters. When she made her first cape and apron, she had to think of the hired girl they had when they moved back to the settlement, and with satisfaction rejoiced that Mattie was not here now to boss her.

When Ellie turned fourteen, another baby was born into the Maust family, but Mama said they did not need a *Maut* this time. Ellie would be able to take the responsibilities of seeing to the household. This new little girl was named Esther. Ellie had plenty to do, what with so many diapers to wash, the cooking to look after, and seeing that everything else was taken care of. The baby seemed to be more fussy than Andy or the twins had been, and Ellie often spent several hours during the night taking care of her new sister. She was glad that since she was the oldest girl of the family, she was needed at home and didn't have to work for someone else.

Ellie looked forward to turning sixteen. Then she would be old enough to begin attending the young folk's singings. These were held on Sunday evening at the home where church services had taken place during the day. First, songs were taken from the German book, and later, English hymns were sung.

After Ellie had been sixteen for about six months, church was held at her house, and she experienced her first evening singing with the other young people. She thoroughly enjoyed it. Several months later, Cora asked her after church if she wanted to come to the singing that evening.

"My brother and I will come by and take you along, if you want to come."

Want to! Oh, yes, she would like nothing better, but she knew she must ask her father.

"Just because you are sixteen now doesn't mean you have to start your *Rum-schpringe* already," said her father. So she didn't go. But by the time she was almost seventeen, she had been to several singings and now was allowed to go almost regularly.

Mrs. Maust was busy working bread dough when she heard a knock at the front porch door.

"Ellie, see who is at the door," she said. "My hands are all doughy."

What a surprise awaited Ellie. When she opened the door, she stood face-to-face with Susie Glick.

"Why, Susie, come in! I sure didn't expect to see you. How have you been?" asked Ellie.

"Just fine," answered Susie. "Is it really you, Bussli? Oh, but I can't call you that anymore. My, how you have grown! And so pretty. I always knew you would be!" Ellie blushed at this remark, but made no comment.

"Oh, hello, Lizzie," Susie addressed Mrs. Maust. "How are you?"

"Alright," answered Mama. "What brings you over here?" She noticed Susie was wearing Conservative Mennonite dress and a covering without ribbons to tie. Her hair was parted slightly on the side.

"Well, I really came to talk to Jake. Is he home?"

"Yes, he and the boys are out in the barn. They were doing some repair work on the hayracks."

"Well, then, maybe I should go out and find him," Susie replied.

"Oh, here he comes now," said one of the twins.

Mr. Maust had seen a car parked in the driveway and thought possibly some salesman had come to see him. You can imagine how surprised he was when he came into the kitchen and saw Susie Glick.

"Hello, Jake," Susie greeted him. "I want to talk with you."

"Well," was all he said.

"Maybe it would be better if we talked in private," she suggested.

"What you have to say can be said right here," Jake grunted.

Susie saw his dislike for her had not changed. "Well," she began, "I came to ask you to forgive me."

"For what?" he asked.

"I'm afraid I did not have a Christian attitude toward you when I worked for you. I even tried to persuade Ellie to do and have things you didn't approve of. That wasn't right. It's been bothering me. Can you please forgive me?" Susie asked, and Ellie observed tears in her eyes.

Jake cleared his throat and mumbled something, but no one understood what he said.

Susie tried again. "It would mean so much to me,

and I want a clear conscience. I know I did wrong,
and I'm sorry. Am I forgiven, then?"

"Yes, yes," said Jake, rather irritably.

"Well, I'll feel better. I'm sorry I acted that way. Is
it all taken care of then?"

Jake didn't say another word, but turned and
walked out of the house.

"Oh, I see you have another baby. Is it a girl or
boy?" asked their former *Maut*.

"It's a girl," answered Ellie. "We named her
Esther."

"I like that," Susie said. "Say, Ellie, why don't you
walk out with me, and we could talk a little yet
before I go. I must leave soon. William is expecting
me home by four."

"Who is William?" asked Ellie.

"Oh, he is my husband. The one who had the fancy
buggy. Remember?" she laughed.

"But now you have a car."

"Yes, we did not join the Old Order. But, Ellie, I
have learned so much, and I understand the Bible
better than I did before. But you just listen to your
parents—and to God. Don't let me or anyone else in-
fluence you. Do only what God tells you in your
heart to do. Have you had any dates yet?" she asked.

"Oh, no," Ellie answered, blushing again.

"Well, you will," she said. "Ellie, I've been so
happy since I married William, and we are both
Christians. Just be sure to get a Christian boyfriend.
The Lord will lead you, if only you ask him to. I must
go now. Maybe we will see each other again. Good-
bye, Ellie."

"Good-bye," answered Ellie. In her mind, Ellie thought Pop would still say, *Susie is some fancy. More so than ever now.*

When Ellie was eighteen, she had her first date. And the words that Susie said came to her: "Do only what God tells you in your heart to do. Be sure to get a Christian boyfriend." And so Ellie grew to womanhood, and wondered about many things.

17

Commotion in the Henhouse

Another summer came and went—with its days of endless canning, gardening, sewing, cleaning, baking, and loads of washing. If Ellie had learned to work as well as her mother, her brothers had learned just as much about farming and caring for the livestock. In fact, the Maust parents were seriously contemplating taking a long-delayed vacation to visit relatives in several different states.

"Do you suppose the family can get along without us?" Lizzie asked her husband. Jake was the one who had been really eager to go.

"I don't know why not," he answered. He assured her that the boys could do just as well as he did with the farm. "Besides, if we go now, we can be home again by corn-husking time. After that will come the butchering for ourselves and helping the neighbors. You know we will just put it off again if we don't go now."

Lizzie saw how much Jake looked forward to seeing his uncles, aunts, and cousins, and she just couldn't say no.

"But I have a few late setting hens," Mama remembered.

"Ach," said Ellie, "I can take care of them. And if I can't take care of the peeps, the mother hens can."

Even Papa laughed at that remark. So it was decided they would leave on the tenth of October.

"We will be taking the two youngest children along. Ellie, you will need to make a few new dresses for Esther to wear on the trip. She grows so fast. Seems I can't keep her and Andy in clothes anymore. Andy will need a couple of shirts, yet, too," said Mama.

"I'll sew them up in the evenings, if need be," answered Ellie.

"Sounds as if you young folks want to get rid of us, as anxious as you seem to see us leave," Lizzie remarked.

"Oh, no! We just feel you and Papa need a rest," they all agreed.

The morning of departure arrived, a bright sunny October day. Roy was to drive Papa, Mama, Andy, and Esther to the train depot, where they would leave for Indiana, their first stop.

"Now, be sure to check those hens twice a day," Mama admonished Ellie. "The chicks should hatch anytime now."

"I will," promised Ellie.

"And, girls, you help good with the work, and mind Ellie."

"Oh, Mom," they answered. "Don't worry. We know."

"Come on, Mama," encouraged Jake. "We don't want to miss the train."

Mama looked back and waved several times. Finally they rounded the bend in the drive and lost sight of the house. She turned and listened to Jake instruct their son about his duties during their absence.

"And just because we are gone, don't think you young folks have to run all over the countryside. Take good care of the horses. Curry them every day. Put the milk check in the bank. We left enough money with Ellie for groceries or whatever you might need."

"You are beginning to sound like Mom," Roy teased.

"It pays to remind you," said Jake. "Just remember whose son you are."

The first day went real well. Jake's youngsters learned a long time before how to get along with each other. They found it was much more pleasant to laugh and show kindness and concern than to quarrel. In their youth, the hickory stick taught them many of these things.

After supper that first night, they decided to sing awhile. They loved singing together. Gathering the hymnbooks, they made their way to the front porch. The three girls sat on the swing, and the boys found a place on the steps. Annie chose her favorite song first.

"We knew it would be 'Take It to the Lord in

Prayer,' " said Sam. Annie just wrinkled her nose at him. They all joined in and sang heartily.

"Let's sing 'In the Sweet By and By,' " requested Sam.

"I knew it," teased Annie. And so they sang on until it was almost too dark to see the words.

"Someone must be burning leaves," remarked Fannie. "I smell smoke."

"It doesn't smell like smoke from leaves," said Roy.

"Listen," Ellie quieted them, "I hear music. It sounds like it's coming from down by the creek. What can it be?"

The big collie dog heard it, too. He perked up his ears, and a low growl escaped from deep within his throat. The boys decided to take their flashlights and do some investigating.

"Be careful," warned Ellie. "Take Shep along."

Ellie and the twins went back into the house and waited. After some time, they heard Shep bark. Then all was quiet. Not even the music could be heard anymore. The girls hoped no harm had come to their brothers. They kept watching for the shine of a flashlight. By and by they saw a small flicker through the tree branches along the lane.

"Here they come," exclaimed Annie, bounding out to the porch to meet them.

"What was it?" all three girls asked in chorus.

"A band of gypsies. They are just sitting around a campfire and playing violins."

"How many are there?" Fannie wondered.

"Oh, maybe twenty-four or so. I didn't count

them. There are some small children in the group, too."

"Do you think they will bother us?" asked Ellie.

"Not tonight, anyway," Roy surmised.

"We had better go to bed. Morning will be here before we know it," Sam said. He was right. The gypsies did not disturb them that evening. Ellie lay awake for a long while, listening to the sweet, plaintive sound of the violins. It made her feel rather sad and lonely, yet it was beautiful, too.

Next morning, Ellie checked first thing to see if the eggs under the setting hens were hatching. She knew even before she lifted the hen from her nest, for she heard soft peeps coming from the corner. Three eggs had hatched in one nest, and one chick from the other batch. She knew that by noon they would probably all be out of the shells.

The girls were just finished with the dishes and Ellie was sweeping the porch when around the bend in their drive came the whole gypsy caravan.

"Quick, Annie, go out to the barn and get the boys," Ellie told her sister.

Annie ran as fast as she could. By the time the long line stopped by their gate, Roy and Sam met them there.

"Lady, come here, lady," requested one of the older gypsy women. She pointed to Ellie. "Come now, I tell your fortune." Ellie didn't move. So the woman walked to the porch where she stood and took her hand. Shep came into view and showed his disapproval.

"Call off dog. I no want trouble. I not hurt you."

Roy called Shep over to his side, but both boys and the dog kept their eyes upon this dark, mysterious woman.

"No," said Ellie, pulling her hand away. "I don't want my fortune told. We do not believe in it."

"Oh, but you pretty girl. I see a happy future for you."

"Only God knows our future. He numbers our days, and our life is in his hands," Ellie told her.

"Well, I see you do not believe gypsy lady. Maybe you buy pretty beads then."

"No, I don't think so," answered Ellie. So engrossed were the five Maust young folks with what the gypsy lady had to say that they didn't notice a few others who had stealthily made their way to the henhouse. All of a sudden, frightened screams filled the air. Shep took off in a flash. The two gypsy men ran from the henhouse under attack by two very angry hens. As if that wasn't enough, the fiesty old rooster was flapping and clawing at one of the men, and Shep grabbed the pant leg of the other one.

Broken eggs were running down their faces from where they had tried to hide some eggs under their hats. Their pants were wet from eggs stashed away in their pockets. When they tried to reach underneath the setting hens, they were hardly even able to get the eggs. The mother hen protected their own.

"Stop them, stop!" yelled the men. "We go now!"

Roy called off the dog, and Sam chased the old red rooster away. The hens returned to their nests and their new babies. It didn't take long for the gypsies to leave and the young folks had a good laugh.

"The little dark-eyed children did look cute, though, didn't they?" Fannie said after they had gone back into the house.

"Yes, they did," answered Ellie. And if they were hungry, I would gladly have given them something to eat, but stealing is wrong."

"Them chickens taught them it doesn't pay to steal, anyway," laughed Annie.

On Monday, there were two letters in the mail. One was from Mom and Papa, and the other was from Missy. Ellie had not heard from Missy once since they moved and had often wondered why. It sounded in the letter as if she had written before, but never received an answer. Ellie wondered at this. What could have happened? Missy was in the hospital at the time of this writing for more surgery on her crippled leg. She wrote only a short note.

The other letter stated that the Maust parents were now about ready to leave Indiana for Iowa, and asked if everything was alright at home. Had the eggs hatched yet? And how were the boys getting along?

That night Ellie answered both letters. Her mother had told her to send the mail to Uncle Enos's in Iowa. That's were they expected to be most of the time. Ellie's letter to Missy was polite, but short, too, as she seemed different somehow just by the way her writing appeared.

Sunday evening after chores, the girls went with their brothers to the singing. They took two buggies, because Roy told them he might not be coming home right afterward.

"Oh, is it Levi's Naomi again?" said Ellie, winking at him.

"Well, it's not David Eash, anyway," answered Roy.

Ellie blushed. She had been seeing quite a good deal of David all summer, and some folks had begun to think it was getting serious.

"Just never you mind," she said. The twins giggled. They thought a lot of David, even if he always teased them.

It was one of the best singings Ellie had ever attended, and her evening with David was an enjoyable one. They had a good laugh when she told him about the gypsies and the setting hens.

"Maybe you should have let the old woman tell your fortune," David said. "Then I wouldn't have to ask you."

"Ask me what?" Ellie questioned.

"To go steady with me," he replied.

"Oh, David, are you serious?"

"I was never more serious in my life. What do you say to that?"

"I'd like to, David," she answered.

"Well then, it's settled," he said.

Two happy people parted that evening with the promise to seek God's will in their lives.

18
A Broken
Circle

Ellie was glad that her parents were home again. Her mother reported that it was nice to visit relatives and friends and see other places, but home was still best. Her father said Mama didn't know how to relax if she wasn't working, but you could tell he, too, was ready to get back into harness, as he put it.

The baby and Andy seemed to have grown in the few short weeks they were gone. Mama said she believed the two little ones had been homesick—because they fussed a lot. Now that everything would be back to normal, Papa said they would start husking corn in a few weeks. It looked like a good crop. The girls would help, as well as the boys. Sam and Roy were two of the best huskers in the area. Pop figured that by working together they could have the corn all in the crib by Thanksgiving.

The women had some apple butter to cook yet and a little winter sewing to do, then work should let up until butchering time. Later it would be their turn to have the church services at their home. That was always a lot of work.

Ellie wondered if she should tell her parents that she and David Eash were going steady. One day when they were working together cleaning the pantry shelves, she decided to tell her mother.

Mrs. Maust was pleased. "I thought maybe you were," said her mother. "David is a nice boy and comes from a good family."

"Should I tell Papa, too?" Ellie questioned.

"Yes, I think so," Mama encouraged her.

Mr. Maust seemed pleased, too. "David is a hard worker from what I have heard, and not so wild, like some. He is old enough to be baptized, I would think. And what about you, Ellie? Aren't you about ready to join the church?"

"Yes, Papa, I've been thinking about it," she answered.

She knew she was older than most girls were when they became members of the church. Perhaps in the spring, when the next group began to receive instruction prior to baptism, she would join the class.

One Saturday evening after supper, the family was gathered in the living room for evening devotions when Papa became very talkative. He was generally a man of few words, but tonight he spoke freely to the family. Jake told them all how he appreciated their obedience in remaining with their parents in the Amish faith, and how much it meant to him that they were such good workers, helping around the farm and the house. He asked that if he had been unfair or wronged any of them, including Lizzie, he might be forgiven. It seemed so strange to have him express himself in this manner.

Ellie couldn't keep it back any longer. She had to know. "Papa, did you ever forgive Susie Glick?"

Papa looked startled. Then he cleared his throat. The room was very quiet. No one knew what to expect. Mama sometimes wished her oldest daughter weren't quite so bold. Then Jake spoke. "Yes, Ellie, I can honestly say I have. That doesn't mean I approve of what she did, but I forgave her."

Ellie felt relieved and happy.

"Yes," said Jake Maust, "I am at peace with God and my fellowman."

The family had their evening prayer. As Ellie retired that night, she felt a closeness and a bond to the others that she had not felt before.

The next day was the between-Sunday, so there was no church. But in the afternoon, some young folks came to the Maust home to go skating on the pond. This was something they frequently enjoyed. David was part of the group, and Ellie noticed what an excellent skater he was. It was a pretty sight to see the rosy-cheeked fellows and girls glide so nimbly across the icy pond.

Then they heard a shout from the direction of the house and saw Mrs. Maust come running across the frozen lawn toward them.

"Come quick," she called and turned back to the house.

Terror struck Ellie, for she had never heard her

mother speak in such a tone. Immediately, she removed her skates and ran for the house. David followed, as did the twins and Roy and Sam.

Lizzie met them at the door. "It's Papa," she said. Fear creased her face. "I can't wake him. He laid down for a nap and said I should wake him at four o'clock, but I can't. I think he is. . . . " She could not say the word. Everyone just stood there. Then Ellie reached for David's hand and led him to the room where her father had gone for his rest. Roy and the twins followed. Sam stayed at his mother's side. It was very silent in that bedroom.

Then the young people returned to the kitchen, where Sam and Mrs. Maust still stood waiting. A low moan escaped Ellie's lips. Mama heard and asked, "Is he?"

"Yes, Lizzie," answered David. "He is gone."

Mama would have fallen had it not been for Roy and Sam. They led her to a chair, and one of the twins brought a cool washcloth for her forehead.

Things happened fast after that. From everywhere, neighbors and friends arrived. Many more young folks came to help with the chores. Roy and Sam told them what to do, but there was not much difference between work at the Maust home and other Amish farms, so there were no problems. Women brought food, and soon the evening meal was on the table. No one in the family was hungry, but out of gratefulness to the concerned friends, they tried to eat.

The body was removed to prepare it for burial, and the family gathered in the living room to make final arrangements. Ellie asked David to join them. He didn't know if he should, but Mrs. Maust assured him that her daughter needed his support at this trying time. So he found a seat beside her and sat in silent meditation for a short while with the bereaved.

Tears flowed freely. When Lizzie Maust could finally speak, she said, "Children, I need your help. We have so many relatives in other states that need to be contacted. I don't know where to begin."

"Shall I see that they get the message?" asked David.

"Oh, would you?" asked Lizzie.

"Yes, I'd be glad to. Just make a list and I'll call them." Ellie, too, was grateful for his help.

The bishop and his wife arrived and were shown into the room where the family had gathered. Together they planned when and where the funeral services would be held, as well as who would be the pallbearers, what text was to be used, and the hymns they wished to have sung. One of the church members had a shop where he made plain caskets.

Ellie slept very little that night. There was an ache in her chest that would not go away.

The body was kept in the home, and many people came for the viewing. In the evening, the young folks came to sing and comfort the Maust household. The morning of the funeral was cold and cloudy. Snow had fallen during the night, and a sharp northeast wind was blowing. The funeral was held at the Maust home, for they had ample room.

At eight-thirty buggies began to come up the lane,

and soon there was a line of them as far as you could see. Mother and the children sat on the benches closest to the casket. Promptly at nine, the service began. The minister reminded everyone that this gathering was not one of their own choosing; but God had planned it thus, and he makes no mistakes. The text was from Hebrews 9:27—"And it is appointed unto men once to die, but after this the judgment."

The minister preached to the living, and no flowery words were spoken about the departed one. The bishop said that because of the life this man had lived, he had good hope for him. "Father's place at the table will now be empty," he continued. "His rocker, too, will be vacant, and his place in the church will leave a great void." This caused much weeping, not only by the family, but by many sympathizing friends. "Father's heart just gave out," the bishop continued, "and now the circle is broken."

One last time, the family looked upon their papa's face, then the casket was closed. It was a slow and cold journey to the grave site. Ellie was concerned about her mother, for she knew that yet another child was on the way. She didn't like to take the chance of Lizzie's catching a cold. But Mrs. Maust seemed unaware of the icy wind and snow that kept falling. The twins were caring for Andy and Esther, so Ellie and Roy stayed close by Mama. She seemed to linger as others began to leave the cemetery, but then she looked around and saw her family shivering in the cold.

"My children need me," Lizzie said. "I must go

on." And she walked toward the waiting buggy.

That night after everyone had gone, Ellie asked, "Mama, would you like me to sleep down here with you?"

"Would you? I need to talk," Lizzie said. They talked way into the night.

"Remember what Papa said to us Saturday night?" asked Ellie. "Do you suppose he knew this was coming?"

"Oh, Ellie," said her mother. "I don't know. But I'm glad he had peace and forgiveness in his heart. And I'm glad, too, we took that trip to visit our relatives. He enjoyed it so much."

After a long silence, she added, "The bishop is right. The circle has been broken. But we are still a family."

Ellie held Mama's hand until sleep came.

19
Baptism
Sunday

Home was never quite the same after Papa was gone. But life went on, and so did the Maust family. The boys were good farmers and went on with the work just like Papa would have done. Mama felt very thankful that she had grown children who faithfully stood by her.

In the spring, another boy was born. "I'll name him Jake," said Mrs. Maust. The rest of the family agreed. They knew their mother was, in a small way, trying to hold onto that which had been taken from her. Little Jake weighed ten pounds at birth, the biggest child Lizzie ever had. She seemed unable to gain her strength back as easily as usual. Her family, however, showered her with consideration.

"Mama," said Ellie one evening, "I would like to join the church this summer."

"I'm so glad," answered Lizzie. "I had hoped you would. You are plenty old enough, you know."

"I know I am, but I needed to be sure that this is what I really want."

"Why, Ellie! What do you mean?" asked her mother.

"Maybe it's wrong for me even to think this way," Ellie began. "But you remember when Susie Glick worked for us?"

"Yes," Lizzie said.

"Well, it's just that she was so *gut miedich* (kind) to me and seemed like a real Christian girl—the kind of girl I want to be. But she didn't stay with our Amish church. Papa thought she was not a good example for me, and that she did wrong by going to another church. But then Mattie Yoder came to work for us, too. She was very strict about church rules. Papa liked her, even if she wasn't as good a worker as Susie, and you know she wasn't nice to us children. It didn't seem like she was Christian at all."

"Oh, Ellie," Mrs. Maust protested. "We must not judge."

"They were so different, and yet both said they were Christians."

"You must understand," Lizzie explained, "that Mattie and Susie are from different families. The Yoders have always been very strict in church discipline. The Glicks, though maybe just as faithful in their worship of God, were more liberal. So who of us can say one is right and the other wrong?

"I know Susie was much more outgoing and pleasant," Lizzie continued, "but I'm sure Mattie thought she was helping by the things she did. Ellie,

I hope you are not thinking of joining another church, like Susie did. Papa and I have always wanted to keep all of our children in the old church, where you were born and raised. Please, Ellie, don't do something you may regret."

"David and I have talked it over already," Ellie said. "He is ready to make a commitment too and be baptized. We both agreed that if any of our parents objected, we would stay Amish. We do want to be obedient. I know that when I was a child, I was strong willed and often rebelled, but now I see things in a different light. Can you forgive me for the trouble I caused and the many anxious moments?"

"Of course, Ellie," answered Lizzie. "Ach, you were just a child then."

There were twelve girls and eight boys in the instruction class, and they all faithfully came each Sunday until baptism day. Some folks said it was the largest such group in the history of their church. Ellie was glad that David and her brother Roy were also in the class with her. They often discussed the previous Sunday's happenings.

Three of the young folks taking the class were rather headstrong and determined to cling to some things against the wishes of the church. Hannah Beachy and Fannie Yoder had a hard time agreeing to wearing longer dresses, as well as combing their hair without any waviness. Elam Hershberger continued to wear sleeve holders and didn't want to take the white rings from his horse's harness.

After five Sundays, the young folks were told that

unless they showed one hundred percent coopera-
tion, the entire class would be denied baptism until
all conformed. This was not done to punish, but with
the hopes that out of consideration for their friends,
those who were causing problems would be willing
to obey. It worked just as the minister had intended.
However, Ellie and David both felt the hearts of
these young folks had not been changed, and it sad-
dened them.

"Do you think it's right to do as the church asks
just to be baptized?" Ellie asked David that evening
on their way to the singing.

"Not as I understand it; it wouldn't be for me. The
way I feel, I want to be baptized because I have
found a new life," David said. "The things I once
enjoyed, I no longer want. There are some details
about the Amish church I may not agree with completely, but it's not worth causing hurt feelings."

"Oh," said Ellie, "that's just the way I feel, too. We
can sacrifice a little for the sake of peace."

One Sunday morning the bishop informed the
group that they would take the voice of the church in
two weeks. If they received a good report, they
would be accepted as members in four weeks.

On the Sunday they took the vote of the congrega-
tion the *Yunga* (young folks) waited anxiously to
find out what the decision of the church would be.
Finally, as they were all assembled in an upstairs
room, the bishop relayed the verdict. It was agreed
to baptize them into church membership in two
weeks. Of course, the bishop added, "If it is the
Lord's will." He always said that because one never

knows what a day may bring.

On baptism Sunday, Roy and Ellie made sure they were neat and presentable. Ellie tried to push her wavy hair back under her covering, but it had a way of its own. Many Amish girls envied her and wished they were so lucky as to have naturally curly or wavy hair. But Ellie knew she must never feel pride.

In the Amish church, the men and women never sit together. But today, after the class had been given its final instructions, the young people filed down from the upstairs room and sat on five benches which were placed end to end. The boys went first. Since Ellie was older than any of the other girls, she led the girls. Thus she sat beside the last boy, who happened to be her brother Roy. She was glad they were seated together for this important event in their lives. She glanced up and saw her mother seated directly across from her. Lizzie had a smile on her face.

The minister began his sermon. Ellie tried to understand the implications of his message. Most of the sermon that day was about obedience and the seriousness of the promises they were making before God and the church.

When the sermon ended, all the applicants were asked to kneel facing forward. Then the bishop asked them one by one, "Are you sorry for your past sins? Do you renounce Satan and the world? Do you promise to abide by the rules and ordinances of the church and remain a faithful member?"

To these, each one answered yes. Then they were asked, "Do you believe that Jesus Christ is the Son of

God?" Ellie's voice trembled slightly as she spoke her vows in this sacred hour.

The deacon of the church stood nearby with a pitcher of water. After each question had been answered and each person confessed Christ as Lord, the bishop began with the row of boys. Cupping his hands upon the first lad's head, he said, "Upon your confession of faith and in the presence of God and his witnesses, I baptize you in the name of the Father, and of the Son, and of the Holy Ghost."

As each name of the triune God was mentioned, the deacon poured a small amount of water into the bishop's cupped hands, who then applied it to the head of the new member. After the eight boys, the girls were baptized in a similar manner. However, the bishop's wife removed each girl's covering until the water had been applied.

After the entire class was baptized, the bishop dried his hands with his clean, white handkerchief. Returning to the first boy's side, he extended his right hand and said, "Arise and, like as Christ has risen from the dead, so should you walk." Then he gave each boy the kiss of fellowship, or the holy kiss, as it is better known. When each boy had been greeted in this manner, the bishop's wife stepped forward again. As the bishop gave each girl the right hand of fellowship, he then presented her to his wife, who kissed her. Everything was quiet during this sacred time in the lives of these young people.

As Ellie took her seat on the bench again, she saw her mother wipe tears from her eyes. She knew they were tears of joy, because she herself had shed a few. Ellie wanted to remember this feeling always and to remain faithful forever.

Her brother glanced at her and smiled slightly. She could tell he was very happy, too. All of a sudden—she didn't know why—Ellie thought of her long-ago friend, Missy. She wondered if Missy had ever been baptized. Years before, Ellie envied her friend for all the things she had—all that a young child could want—the modern conveniences, the pretty clothes. But now Ellie wouldn't have traded places with her for anything.

David went to the Maust home for supper that evening. Roy's girlfriend was also invited, as were some of the twins' friends. The girls set out a fine meal of potato salad, sliced ham, cheese, and a large dish of radishes and pickles. There were two kinds of pie and tall glasses of homemade lemonade. What a pleasant evening it was.

Lizzie Maust sat quietly by with a faraway look in her eyes.

"Mama, you must be thinking about something very important," Fannie broke in on her thoughts. "Dena has asked you to pass the salad three times."

"Ach, my, I should mind my business more," answered Lizzie quickly. She picked up the salad bowl and handed it to Dena.

"What were you thinking about, anyway?" Ellie inquired.

"Oh, just that I'm so glad for the *Yunga* who were baptized today." She looked at the fine group around her table. "I wish Papa could have been with us today. He would have been glad, too."

20
Ellie's
Wedding Day

No more letters came from Missy, and Ellie often wondered whatever became of her. Even though she now felt that her friend had been rather worldly, she wished her well. That was the way she had been brought up, Ellie reasoned. Missy had been born into an English home and Ellie into an Amish one, and that was that.

Just because Ellie had become a church member and a Christian did not mean she had no more temptations. Many times she struggled with difficult problems. One of these was trying to feel kindly toward some of the younger Amish boys and girls. They came to Sunday evening singings sometimes just to act up, it seemed to her.

Several times when the new church members were made fun of, Ellie spouted off to David about it on their way home.

"Ellie," David said one night, "some of them show

a little too much spunk. But don't let it bother you. They'll get over it. It's just a spell they're going through."

"Do you really think so?" Ellie asked timidly, ashamed that she had shown such a display of emotion.

"Yes, I do," said David. "Anyway, we may not be going to the singings too much longer, if a certain spunky girl I know will say yes to what I'm going to ask her."

"What do you mean?" Ellie wanted to know.

"Dad just bought the Raber place over south of the Twenty. He wants me to farm it for him. There is a nice house on it, and I'd surely need someone to cook and keep house for me. I know of no one I'd rather share it with than you. Ellie, will you marry me?"

Goose bumps ran down Ellie's arms. She knew someday she wanted to hear David ask her that question. But now, all of a sudden, she was speechless.

"Well," said David, "where has all that spunk gone?"

"Don't tease about something like this. Are you serious?"

"I was never more serious in my life, and I'm waiting for an answer," David replied.

"Could I talk it over with Mother?" asked Ellie.

"Sure you can," David answered. "Your mother is such a good woman, and I wouldn't want to upset her in any way. But could you give me an answer by next Sunday?" Ellie said she would let him know by then.

Mrs. Maust was not surprised at what her oldest daughter had to tell her on Monday morning. She had been expecting this news for some time. "Do you have any time set?" Lizzie asked.

"No, Mama, David only asked me last night, and I told him I wanted to talk with you about it first. I didn't want to make any plans unless they suited you."

"David is one of the nicest boys I know," Lizzie said, "and I'll be well satisfied if you marry him. Maybe this fall would be a good time. We will need to know as soon as possible. Oh, my, there will be so much to do!"

"Yes, Mama, I know, but we girls are all good workers. As soon as I'm through working at Levi Helmuth's, I'll stay home." Since Ellie turned twenty, she had been working as a hired girl for different Amish families. She was a good *Maut* and much in demand. Often she thought of the difference in the two hired girls her parents had employed when she was a young child. This helped her to remember to be kind and cheerful in many different situations.

Ellie seemed to be walking on air all week long. There was a spring in her step and a song in her heart, as she eagerly awaited the weekend.

Sunday singing was at Cora's house, Ellie's best friend. Ellie would not have gone, but since it was at Cora's house, she decided she should.

"Let's not stay late at the singing tonight, David," Ellie said soon after they were on their way.

"That's fine with me," he answered. Ellie knew he could hardly wait to hear what she had to tell him.

They stayed and sang with joy in their hearts all through the familiar German hymns, but after two songs in the English language, Ellie nodded toward David and left the place at the table where she had been sitting.

Cora noticed and followed. "Are you leaving already?" she asked. "Aren't you enjoying yourself, or don't you feel good?"

"Yes, Cora, we are leaving. I've had a good time, and I feel fine. You are my best friend, so I know I can trust you. David and I have something very special to talk about and just want plenty of time."

"Oh, Ellie," Cora exclaimed, "I'm so happy for you. David is really a nice boy. I know you will have a good man."

"Please don't tell anyone about this," Ellie requested.

"No, no," promised Cora, "I won't."

When an Amish couple plans to marry, they try to keep it a secret and pretend it's the furthest thing from their minds. The wedding is made known to the public only two weeks before the marriage takes place. The bishop announces it at church services.

"David's driving up to the front gate. I must go now," Ellie told Cora as she headed out the door and down the walk.

They had not gone far in their buggy when David asked the question Ellie knew he would. She felt some of her former little-girl antics return and had an urge to pretend she wasn't sure yet and needed more time. But she saw by the moonlight the eager expression on his face and sensed the anxious tone of his voice. She couldn't keep him in suspense any longer.

"Yes, David, I would like very much to be your wife." She knew those were the words he wanted to hear. "I just hope I'll make you a good *Frau*" (wife, or woman).

"I'm sure not worried about that," David said, kissing her lightly. "Do you have any idea when we could get married, Ellie?"

"Well, Mother and I thought this fall would be alright. But we didn't set any special date. Do you have any certain day in mind, David?"

"Well, if it were all up to me, I'd say tomorrow," he said laughing.

"Oh, you! There's no way I could get ready that fast."

"I know. I was just teasing. You women always act like you have to do a year's work to get ready."

"It's lots of work," Ellie said. "But I'll gladly do it."

They talked way into the night. They agreed on Thanksgiving as their wedding day.

Now work and plans at the Maust home began in earnest. But, of course, the reason for all the activity had to be kept secret by the family. Mrs. Maust pieced a quilt for Ellie and invited Ellie's friends and cousins. She told them that Ellie never had a quilt of her own, and that it was about time she had one because she had helped so faithfully at home. And so the pretense went on and on. The quilters smiled and exchanged knowing glances. It was an enjoyable quilting day. By evening, Ellie's lovely blue and white tumbling-block quilt was finished. Even the binding was done.

Mrs. Maust and the girls did a lot of extra canning that summer. By fall, Ellie had a nice selection of fruits and vegetables for her and David to use the first year of their marriage. David's folks were giving them a quarter of beef and a whole hog all worked up into hams, sausage, bacon, and pork chops. The beef would provide good hamburgers, steaks, and stew meat. They certainly wouldn't go hungry, David said.

Now Ellie and her sisters were busy sewing. An Amish girl's wedding dress is blue. So are her attendants' dresses. The dresses are all made alike, too, but the bride's is a darker shade. The capes and aprons are made of white organdy. All the girls wear black caps until after the wedding. Then the bride, returning to her house where the meal is served, replaces her black head covering with a white one.

Finally, the day came when the bishop announced that David Eash and Ellie Maust were to be married on Thanksgiving Day. David and Ellie had both been at church that day but left just before the news of their upcoming wedding was made known. This was the custom. Everyone guessed why the couple was leaving in such a hurry.

Now David spent more time at Ellie's home than he did at his. He helped Roy and Sam get the barn cleaned and ready to shelter the many horses that would be there for the big event. He even helped some with cleaning around the outside yard by the pond. But he and Ellie made more than one trip to the house in which they would be living. That's where they would spend their first night, because, as is also the Amish custom, they would not be going on a honeymoon. When they married, they would settle right down to farming, housekeeping, and raising a family.

The day before the wedding, much food was prepared. The Amish bake their own wedding cakes. Since around 275 guests were invited to Ellie's wedding, a lot of cake was needed. There were puddings to prepare and chickens to butcher. David helped with food preparation too. Evening finally came and the whole house was sparkling clean. The cellar and springhouse were overflowing with good food.

The tables had been set up for the couple and their attendants. The bride and groom always sit at a corner table, their attendants on either side. Ellie's twin sisters were her attendants. David's brother, Mose, and one of his cousins from Iowa were the twins' partners. Ellie's best friend, Cora, and her boyfriend would be head table waiters. They would serve the bridal couple's table. Roy and his girl were also table waiters.

Sam was the main "hostler." He would take the couple to the wedding ceremony and bring them back again in his own buggy. Two of David's sisters were also table waiters, and one of his best friends escorted the attendants to and from the wedding.

Thanksgiving Day dawned bright and clear, but it looked like a winter wonderland. Snow had fallen during the night, and it clung to every tree and shrub and fence as far as one could see. As Ellie looked out the window, she prayed within herself:

May my life as David's wife be as clean, pure, and beautiful as this scene before me now. May I never do anything to grieve him or cause him to regret this day. Guide our steps, Lord, that we may build a Christian home and be a real credit to our church and the community in which we live.

Then she dressed and hurried downstairs.

"You are not helping with chores, or anything today, sis," Roy greeted her. "No, sir, this is your day."

"Well, you'll spoil me yet," Ellie told him.

"Oh, don't do that," Sam chided. "David will have his hands full as it is, once she gets that Amish dander up."

"You boys are the limit. Maybe, now just maybe, I'm glad I'm leaving this bunch," Ellie laughed.

Mother came up from the basement where she had gone to check things again and make sure nothing had been overlooked.

"Didn't you sleep well?" asked Ellie. "You look so tired."

"Ach, well, Ellie, you know me. When there is excitement, I can't sleep; but I will, once this is over."

Soon after breakfast many of Ellie's aunts, David's mother, and some of David's aunts began to arrive. These were the cooks, who needed to come early to peel potatoes, fry chicken, make the stuffing, and the like, for the three meals that would be served this day. The noon meal is always the largest—the main meal. Then, after the couple have opened their gifts and much visiting and some singing is done, a lighter evening meal is served.

Many of the older people with families leave after

supper because they have chores to do at home. The young folks spend the evening singing. At midnight, another meal is served. At this time, the young folks pair off, and each boy escorts the girl of his choice to the table and eats with her. The girls often pretend shyness and reluctantly pull back, whereupon several boys assist the young fellow to take her to the table and seat her. It is all a jolly good time.

By nine o'clock, everyone had arrived at Ellie's neighbor's place where the wedding was to take place. Ellie and David had gone early to meet with the ministers in an upstairs room. There they were counseled in the duties of a wife to her husband, and also the husband's duties to his wife.

After this, the couple and attendants made their way downstairs, where six chairs had been placed in the center of the room for them. After the singing of the third hymn, the ministers came from the upper room and found their seats. Now the preaching service began. Ellie listened intently, as did David. The sermon seemed to be especially for them, but nothing impressed Ellie as much as the words of her beloved bishop.

"Today," he began, "is a happy day for you two, and so it should be. But remember, the day will come when you must part in death. Therefore, live your life together so that when that day comes, you will have no regrets of having made this decision of becoming one."

Ellie couldn't help it: two big tears trickled down her cheeks and dropped upon her white apron. Why, those were almost the same words Mama had spoken to her earlier. David noticed her tears and her bowed head and longed to comfort her. No doubt she was thinking of her departed papa.

Mrs. Maust told the other women that she didn't think she had the time to go to see her daughter married, what with all the cooking, the setting of tables, and so on. But everyone encouraged her and David's mother to go. So at eleven-thirty they left the kitchen and headed to the neighbor's place to witness the marriage of their son and daughter. Ellie saw them walk in across the porch, and it made her day complete.

Traditionally, Amish couples marry at exactly twelve noon. The minister asks the questions common in all marriages, to which they answer affirmatively. He joins their hands together and pronounces them man and wife. There are no wedding bands. The couple return to their seats. After the last hymn is begun, the attendants and the couple leave for the bride's home and the wedding feast.

Ellie and her attendants had left their wraps and outer bonnets on a closed-in porch earlier that morning when they arrived for the wedding ceremony. As they hurriedly prepared to leave, Ellie found to her dismay that someone had played a prank on her. Her bonnet strings were knotted so tightly together that she could not get away quickly. Her sister Annie said, "Here, Ellie, take mine. I'll get these knots out." So the joke wasn't on her after all.

Ellie was now a married woman. If she lived to be one hundred, she thought, she would never forget any part of this wonderful day!

21
An Unexpected Visitor

Because Ellie had saved most of her money since she became of age, she and David had furnished their new house very nicely. The day after the wedding, David and Ellie went to help clean up and put everything back in its place. Mrs. Maust looked much more rested, and she assured them she could now sleep again.

"Yeah, but just think," said David, "you have more girls waiting to get married." Then he added, "Right, Fannie?"

The twin made a face at him and pretended to chase him out of the house. Mrs. Maust only smiled and said, "Ach, I'll get a lot of sleep before that happens." Even though both of the twins had steady boyfriends, their mother didn't think they would get married for a few years yet. At least, she hoped they wouldn't.

David's father had given them a cow, and Ellie's

family parted with a dozen hens and a few roosters. Besides that, each family provided a few nice pieces of furniture. So Ellie and David had plenty of rich milk and all the eggs they could use. And with all the canned goods on their pantry shelves, they lived well. Ellie very much enjoyed being a housewife and a homemaker. She loved having family and friends come to visit and often invited them for meals. She was an excellent cook, and enjoyed pleasing David.

The crops did well that first year. Since David and his father were farming on shares, it meant money in their pockets for both of them. David bought himself some feeder pigs and four young heifers. He also bought some shop tools and began making furniture on the side. This was something he loved to do, and he did excellent work. Before long, orders began pouring in as the Amish learned of his skill. He set up shop in a building next to the washhouse. It had been used before only as a storage shed. Ellie helped him clean it out and get it ready for work. In the summer, there was not much going on there. But when winter came, they built a good fire in the stove that had been set up, and the shed became a busy, cozy workshop.

Ellie often stained and varnished for David, putting the finishing touches on the products he made. Even so, Ellie found she still had time on her hands. One day she approached her husband with a new idea.

"David," she said, "I like helping you in the shop, and I try to keep a neat house. But somehow there are days when I don't seem to have enough to do."

"Well," laughed David, "maybe I could teach you how to make furniture. Or, better still, maybe I could turn the farming over to you, so I could spend all of my time in the shop."

"Oh, you! Wait until you hear what I have in mind. That empty room off to the side of the kitchen—well, I just thought, if you don't care, maybe I could make it into a little dry goods store. I could sell notions, too, like pins, buttons, baby things, and—"

"Hold on, there," David interrupted. "Where would you get the money to buy all the things to start with?"

"Have you forgotten the savings I had when we married? And I've managed to put back some egg and milk money. Also, remember, I told you I've been selling more butter in town lately."

"Oh, yes," said David. "I had forgotten your little nest egg. Well, if you are sure that's what you want and that it's not too much for you—okay, go ahead."

Ellie was so grateful. In the next few weeks, David took time to help Ellie set up her place of business. He measured and sawed and hammered, putting up shelves and building counter spaces for her. Ellie painted the room a cheerful light green and made snowy white curtains for the windows.

"I sure appreciate your help," Ellie told David.

"Turnabout is fair play," he answered, remembering how Ellie worked to help him set up his workshop.

Ellie hired an English man to drive a van to take her to Camden, where she knew Borsky had a large warehouse of dry goods. Mr. Morris, the owner of the van, was well known among the Amish as a good source of transportation. He knew his way around in most any city and state. His rates were fairly reasonable, so he was much in demand. Ellie was fortunate to get him on such short notice. They left early in the morning. When they returned at ten-thirty, the van was loaded with bolts and bolts of material and bric-a-brac of all kinds.

David came from the barn just as the van pulled into the driveway. When he saw the stacks of material and the other purchases his wife brought home, he couldn't help but tease her again. "Are you sure you didn't move Borsky's warehouse here?" he asked.

"Don't pay any attention to him, Mr. Morris," said Ellie. "He is always teasing me."

Mr. Morris and David helped carry bundle after bundle inside. Ellie thanked them both and paid Mr. Morris his fare. Hurrying into the kitchen, she grabbed an apron and put it on over her good dress. Then she put the teakettle on to boil.

"What are you doing?" asked David, who had followed her. "I thought you would be anxious to get your store all set up and things put away like you want them."

"Oh, I am," his wife answered. "But it's almost lunchtime. I promised myself if I am allowed to operate a little store from my house, you and our home shall never be neglected because of the little business I run on the side." And they never were. Ellie kept that promise faithfully.

News of the new store at the David Eash home spread, and soon Ellie had a thriving business going. Women asked for shawls, men's long underwear, *Vindel Satchely*, and other items Ellie had forgotten, so she stocked up on whatever her customers asked for. The only times her store closed were the two weeks before church was held at the Eash home, the Christian holidays, and a half day on Saturdays.

David and Ellie did not always agree on everything. They had their ups and downs but were always willing to ask each other's forgiveness and work things out. Ellie still helped David during the winter in his shop. He now made caskets for Amish burial needs. These were plain, with wooden handles. Ellie would varnish them and line the insides with a plain white batiste material.

The years came and went. After almost four years of marriage, a little son came to live with David and Ellie. They had never known such joy, and the responsibilities of raising a child seemed almost overwhelming. But they committed the child to the Lord and prayed for guidance, trusting the one who promises never to forsake.

Several years later, a daughter, and then another son, was born to them. They were busier now but worked well together, and Ellie seemed so well organized that she managed easily. When the babies were born, she had a *Maut*, who also minded the store whenever anyone stopped by to make a purchase. The Amish girls liked working for Ellie and David, so she never had a problem getting help.

Her twin sisters were married now and had

houses of their own. Roy and Sam were also married. Mrs. Maust and her younger children seemed to manage the farm as before. Ellie sometimes worried that her mother did too much. But Mama always told her, "Don't worry about me, Ellie. I find work is my best friend here on earth."

So Ellie tried to agree with David's comment: "Mama knows what she can stand."

Ellie could tell that Mrs. Maust was pleased with all her grandchildren, but somehow Ellie's oldest held a special place in her heart. They had named him Jacob, after Lizzie's husband. But Ellie called him Jake, just like her papa was called. She thought he resembled his grandfather, too.

One day as Ellie was sitting on the porch with her children helping them shell peas from the garden, she saw a car come up the drive. *Wonder who that could be,* she thought. *Probably someone who wants to see David about having some furniture made this winter.*

The car pulled to the gate and stopped. Ellie saw it contained a woman and two children. The lady got out and walked to the other side of the car to open the door for her children. The woman walked with a limp. Ellie dropped her pan of peas. She gasped.

"Mama, what's the matter?" asked Laura, her little girl. "Are you alright?"

"Yes, I'm alright," answered Ellie. Could it be, she thought.... Was it really...? She started toward the gate, where the lady and her children waited.

"Ellie Maust?" the English woman asked.

"Missy!" exclaimed Ellie. "Missy, is it really you?"

"Yes, it's me, really," Missy said as Ellie unlatched the gate. They shook hands.

"Come on in," Ellie invited.

"But I don't want to keep you from your work."

"Oh, no, that's alright—the children will finish what we were doing."

"These are your children? You have three?" asked Missy. "My children wouldn't know how to skin those things," she said, referring to the pea shelling.

Ellie laughed. She had never heard it stated in such a way before. Wait until she told David they were "skinning peas." But Missy had never been taught about such work. "Yes," said Ellie, opening the screen door as they entered her kitchen. "We have three children: Jake, Laura, and Benny. They are a pleasure and are good little workers."

"Well, I just have two, and sometimes I'd like to give them away."

Ellie was shocked. Surely her friend couldn't mean that. How could a mother want to give up her own children?

"Here, have a seat," Ellie said, pointing to a chair.

"Thanks," and Missy sat down. "You sure keep a clean house," Missy commented. "How do you do it with a husband and three kids?"

Ellie had never referred to her children as kids. However, she answered politely that her children had been taught to work from a young age. They had learned that in a happy family there's a place for everything and everything in its place, a responsibility to parents and each other, and a need to live honest, orderly lives.

Missy changed the subject. They talked about their school days, laughing together over many of their shared memories. "I used to wish I could wear a brown dress like yours," Missy said. "Do you remember the pictures Miss Olive, our first-grade teacher, used to put up on the wall when we had colored nicely?"

"Yes, I remember," Ellie said. "Why do you ask?"

"Well, the one with a lamb in a pasture field that had the girl with the brown dress—it was my picture. I remember you did not like it because you thought someone did it to make fun of you. But I did it, imagining it was me in your brown dress."

Ellie laughed. "I remember. And would you believe it, Missy? I used to like your yellow dress so well, I colored my girl's dress yellow."

"Are your parents still living?" Missy asked. "I remember your father was mean."

"No," said Ellie, "my father isn't living anymore. And he was never mean. He may have seemed so to you, but he really wasn't."

Missy's children were getting restless, so Ellie brought out a toy box with wooden blocks and a wooden barn and animals David had made. There was a rag doll with no face, dressed just like Ellie was dressed as a little girl. Ellie thought the children would enjoy these toys, but they soon began fighting over them. Missy told them to stop, but they didn't pay any attention to her. "If you kids don't behave, I'll kill you," she said with exasperation.

Ellie couldn't believe she heard correctly. She was

glad her own children were out of earshot.

"Would you like to see my little store?" Ellie asked.

"You have a store, too?" Missy showed surprise.

"Yes," said Ellie, "it's right here in my house." And she led the way through the kitchen again.

"Oh, how quaint," Missy exclaimed. "Don't you sell any print or flowered material?"

"No," said Ellie, "just plain. That's what our people wear."

"I used to wish I was Amish when I was small," Missy mused. "But now I'm sure glad I'm not."

Missy's children begged for everything from cough drops to plastic tumblers, which Ellie had on display. Missy kept saying, "If you little brats don't shut up, I'll smack you good." But she never did, and she bought them anything they wanted. Ellie had thought of inviting them to stay for lunch, but she wasn't sure she wanted to now.

"It's nice you can run a store like this in your home for your people," Missy said as they returned to the living room. "May I ask you a question that has bothered me for a long time?"

"Sure," Ellie said. "What is it?"

"Why didn't you answer my letters?"

"I only got one, and I did answer it," Ellie told her.

"Well, I wrote you a lot of times. Someone must have got them before you did and destroyed them, and I can pretty well guess who it was."

Ellie knew she was referring to her papa, and she wished Missy would not blame him for it now. She knew her father meant to do what was best for her.

Ellie's children were finished shelling peas and brought them in bowls to the kitchen. The visiting children were fighting again, and the three Eash children watched in amazement.

"If all you little beasts are going to do is fight," their mother exclaimed, "we are leaving." She grabbed her little boy by the arm none too gently and, leaving scattered toys on the floor, headed for the door.

"Mommy, I want a drink," begged her little girl.

"Well, hurry up, then. Where is your faucet?" she asked Ellie.

"Oh, here, I'll get you a glass. We get the water from the pump here at the kitchen sink."

"How quaint," Missy remarked again. She filled the glass and handed it to her little girl. The boy decided he wanted it and grabbed it from his little sister's hand. The glass fell to the kitchen floor and shattered.

"That's it, that's it," Missy said. "We are leaving right now." And with two screaming children, she headed for the car. "My nerves are just shot," she said. "I've got to have a smoke to calm them." She reached into her purse, took out a cigarette, and lit it. "I know you don't approve, Ellie, but trying to cope with these two kids alone is more than I can bear."

"Oh, I'm sorry," Ellie said. "I didn't know your husband wasn't living."

"Oh, he's living, alright," Missy said, "but not with me. He is in the army. He has it easy, I'd say. Well, I'd better be going."

Ellie followed her to the car.

"Oh, who is that?" Missy asked, as she saw David coming from the field.

"Why, that's David, my husband. I'm not Ellie Maust anymore. I'm Ellie Eash now. I like that name, and I like being David's wife and the mother of his children."

"I'm glad you're happy, Ellie."

"Well, see you around, kiddo," was all Missy said as she drove away.

Ellie returned to the house to clean up the broken glass and see that the toys were picked up and put away, but she found her own children had things back in order.

"Mama," asked Laura, "why didn't that woman like her children? And why was she so cross?"

"Oh, Laura, I don't really know."

"Who was it, anyway?" asked David.

"It was Missy," answered Ellie.

"Your old school friend you told me about so often?" David asked.

"Yes, David, my old school friend. I don't want to talk about it anymore. I want to remember us as we used to be—me, a little Amish girl, and my special friend, Missy."

But the family often talked, after the unexpected visit, about how one "skins peas."

Ellie was glad her father had enough wisdom to know what could come of being too friendly with people outside their own group. She appreciated him and her own family more than ever.

22
The
Dawdy Haus

David and Ellie were blessed with one more baby girl. They decided to name her Rebecca, but she always went by the name of Becky.

Ellie couldn't believe how fast her children were growing up. Sometimes it almost frightened her. Soon they would be going to singings and other get-togethers with young folks their own age. Had they been taught well enough, she wondered, to withstand the many temptations confronting today's youth? She sincerely hoped so. She intended to remain an example to them all her life both by word and deed.

Ellie knew a mother's prayers are important. She prayed daily for each of her children. Although accustomed to silent prayer, as the Amish mostly are, still she was sure the Lord knew her heart, her longings, concerns, and desires better than she herself did.

The Eash children loved to sing as much as their parents did. Many evenings before retiring, they gathered around the kitchen table and sang favorite hymns together. Even Becky, at a very young age, joined in with the rest of the family. There was a closeness here that would not easily be broken.

David's dairy had grown from one cow and four heifers to fifteen good Guernsey cows. He also had about twenty pigs. The henhouse was full of chickens. Yet there were times in the winter when there just wasn't enough work to keep one man and two husky boys busy.

"Ellie," David asked one evening, "what would you say about moving closer to Hatfield again?"

"What?" said Ellie, startled.

"How would you feel about moving closer to Hatfield? You know, close to where you grew up."

"I know what you asked me."

"Then why did you ask me to repeat it?" laughed David.

"Because, I just couldn't believe that's what you said," she answered. "Why, David?"

"There just doesn't seem to be enough work here to keep us busy the year round. My dad told me the other day that my youngest brother, Joe, would like a chance to farm this place on shares now."

"But why Hatfield? And what about your shop? And, oh, David, our children will start their *Rumschpringe* and there are so many more temptations near a larger town. They would need to drive so far for singings. Are you sure it would be wise?"

"I get the feeling you are opposed to the idea. I

didn't say we are moving there. I just want to know what you think. I found out in town today that a two-hundred-acre farm with good buildings is for sale over there. I can move my shop tools, if that's what you're worried about. And you know I'd make room for your store. The children would get used to the place soon enough."

"Not too many people would drive that far to come to my store. They could buy most of the same things at Harper's Five and Ten right here in Springdale, even if they have to pay a little more," Ellie reasoned.

"Yes, but at Harper's they couldn't visit with you and exchange news of who is getting married, who has a new baby, and all the neighborhood gossip," David teased.

"There you go teasing again, and I don't think it's funny," Ellie said, fighting back tears.

When David saw how upset his wife was, he apologized and told her he would not insist upon the move.

"Let's talk it over with my mother," Ellie suggested. "She raised her family for many years away from the settlement. Maybe she would give us some advice on whether or not she would recommend it."

David thought that was a good idea. So the next time they went "over home," as they referred to it whenever they visited Lizzie, they brought the subject up with her.

Mrs. Maust looked so tired of late. She was almost completely white-haired now, and her eyesight seemed to be failing her. She sat in her favorite rocker and listened to what David had to say. When he had finished speaking, she smiled.

"Well, I don't know as I could recommend it. But if you feel that's what you really want, and that it's the best for you, then I can't discourage you either. And, Ellie, it's your place to go with your husband and stand by him, even if you'd rather stay here in the settlement."

"Yes, Mama," was all Ellie said. She could have cried, she was so disappointed. It had never entered her mind that her mother would tell David to go if he felt it was best for them. She remembered how reluctant Lizzie had been when Papa brought up the subject of leaving the little village of Springdale and the settlement.

Ellie thought of how attached she had become to her friend Missy, and how Missy had changed. What if they had stayed at Hatfield until she and Missy were both grown? Would she have stayed Amish?

What about her own daughters, if they moved away? Ellie could already see much of her own strong-willed spirit and spunk in little Becky. The thought of exposing her children to worldliness such as she had seen at the English school frightened her. Then she heard her mother ask David why he wanted to move to Hatfield.

"I don't really want to, but my youngest brother wants to farm on shares with Dad. And I don't really have enough work for the boys summer and winter. I'd much rather stay in the settlement, but there just doesn't seem to be any place around here for sale or rent. I found out about a two-hundred-acre place near Hatfield with good buildings that I could get."

"Well, now," said Mama, "maybe the Lord is taking this way to answer my prayer."

What a strange thing to say, Ellie was thinking. *Why would Mama pray that they move to Hatfield?*

"What?" asked David, himself astonished.

"As you know, Jake, Jr., is going with a girl from Illinois. They plan to get married the last of February. But now, don't let the cat out of the bag. They don't want it made known yet," Lizzie said.

"That will leave Esther and me all alone," she continued, "and I'm getting to where I can't help chore too well anymore. We thought we would just have to rent the fields out for share-crop farming. But I just thought, if you need a place, what do you think of building a *Dawdy Haus* (grandparents' small house) for Esther and me, and moving your family here into the big house and farm? I'd sell you the place, or rent it, whatever you would like. That ought to give your boys all the work they can handle, and you could still do your shop work. There are enough outbuildings, so there is no lack of space."

David looked at his wife. "Well, what do you think now?" he asked. He saw by the sparkle in her eyes that Ellie approved.

"I'd like it," she answered, "but I don't believe I could go on with my store here and take care of the big house, the garden, and the yard. It's much bigger than where we are living now."

"Do you mind giving up the store?" Mama wanted to know.

"Well, I may miss it at first, but I'd sure rather let it go and move over here than keep it and go clear off to Hatfield."

"If you plan on giving it up anyway, Esther would probably take over for you. She has often said she would like that kind of business. It would be right here at home, where she could be with me and help along."

Everything seemed to be working out so well, to the satisfaction of all of them. David's children were excited about moving onto the old homeplace, as they called it. Esther was thinking just where she would have her store and how she would fix it. Ellie could plan ahead who would have which bedroom upstairs, and even how she would arrange her furniture, because she remembered every room, wall, and window as if she had left there only yesterday.

Ellie's sisters said that when moving time came, they wanted to help. So did David's family. Ellie knew there would be plenty of willing workers to lighten the task. But first, of course, the *Dawdy Huus* must be built. It would consist of two bedrooms, a kitchen, and dining area combined with a rather large living room. It would connect to the large house through a closed-in hallway. Both bedrooms would have large walk-in closets. The kitchen included lots of storage space. And off to the side of the kitchen, a room would be built for the dry goods store. Construction of the *Dawdy Haus*, would begin as soon as possible to be finished sometime in February.

When word got around that Mrs. Maust wanted

to put up a *Dawdy Haus*, her many friends planned a "frolic." The building began the middle of January, and then it was announced at church that on the following Thursday, weather permitting, there was to be a frolic to put up the *Dawdy Haus* for Mrs. Maust. When Thursday came, a big snowstorm came along with it. So the work had to be postponed, and a new date was set for the following Tuesday. But Tuesday still was cold, snowy, and windy. Then on Saturday the sun shone brightly, so neighbors came from miles around. The men were equipped with hammers, nails, and saws. The women came bringing pots and bowls of food, and cakes, pies, and puddings of all kinds to feed the hungry workers. One man was overseer and directed the work so things would run smoothly and be done right. The Amish are known for the quality of their work, and each one did his best.

"How many crooked nails did you drive today?" Ralph Zook asked Sam Maust.

"They were all straight when I started. And by the time I finished, the wood covered all but their heads, so I really can't tell you," Sam answered.

The weather was still cold, but the fellowship was warm and friendly. How Ellie enjoyed these times with her people. For a brief moment, she thought of Missy. She must remember to pray for her. Ellie felt almost selfish for growing up in an Amish home and community. God had been good to her. Her father had certainly been right when he said, "As the twig is bent, so grows the tree."

By evening, the small house was built and under

roof. Everyone left with a good feeling of accomplishment and satisfaction.

The following week Esther and her mother began to varnish the woodwork and paint the walls. They left the door to the hallway and large house open for ventilation. After the painting was finished, they began the clean-up work. Ellie and her girls came often to help. David and the boys put up shelves in the new store. They built extra counter and storage space because Ellie mentioned that she hardly had enough places to put things when her business grew.

"Women never have enough room for all their stuff," said Jake, Jr. "Give them a silo and they would fill it to the top and want more room."

"Oh, Jake, you are just like your brother-in-law," said Ellie, "always teasing."

"Well, we have to do something to keep you women in hand and liven things up a bit, don't we, David?"

"I've learned to go a little bit easy on the teasing part," David replied in mock fear. They all laughed, and another fun-filled day soon ended.

Mrs. Maust held a small sale to dispose of the many items she would no longer need. The *Dawdy Haus* would not hold as much furniture as the large one she was living in did. Many items were purchased by her own children, who needed them for their growing families. Things sold well. After David bought the homeplace, Lizzie and Esther moved into the new house, where they lived very comfortably.

Ellie was glad when her own moving day was

done. Her mind went back to that other time when their *Maut*, Mattie, tried to tell her what she could or couldn't do. This time, moving was a joy. Ellie gave her oldest daughter, Laura, the room which held so many memories for herself. Maybe someday Ellie would share some of the stories with her, but for now she would just enjoy being a mother and homemaker on the old homestead.

Tired as they were that first night in their new home, Ellie and her family gathered around the kitchen table and sang for a little while before going to bed. Grandma Maust and Esther joined in. What a happy time they had, and somehow Ellie knew it was only the first of many more to come.

Ellie looked around the table at her husband and her own four children, then at her mother and youngest sister. She looked out the window facing the pond—here is where she had grown to womanhood, and here she would live out her days.

Tears of joy welled up in Ellie's eyes. She was thankful, and she was content. The Lord had truly blessed her.

The Author

Mary (Christner) Borntrager was the seventh of ten children born to Amish parents in a rural setting near Plain City, Ohio, in 1921.

Initially, her education ended after eight years in the public school. Later she attended teacher training institute at Eastern Mennonite College, Harrisonburg, Virginia. Then she taught at a Christian day school for seven years.

She married John Borntrager at the age of nineteen. Their children are Jay, Kathryn (Keim), John T., and Geneva (Massie). After her children were grown, she earned a certificate in Childcare and Youth Social Work from the University of Wisconsin. She then worked with emotionally disturbed children and youth for twelve years.

Mary has written short stories and poems over the years. Her husband, John, encouraged her to write about "Ellie" and was thrilled when word came that it was accepted for publication by Herald Press. But cancer had already invaded his body and he did not survive to see the finished book.

Mary lives in a retirement village in Central Ohio, where she enjoys visits from her children and eleven grandchildren. She is a member of Hartville Mennonite Church and draws strength and comfort from the Bible and from her church community. She also enjoys quilting, reading good books, writing poetry, and embroidering.

She hopes this book will clarify some misunderstandings about the Amish and that it will provide some useful perspectives for those who read it.